I0817622

SANCTA SANCTORUM
GILBERT GALLO
TRANSLATED BY GIULIA DE GASPERI

Published by Outland Entertainment LLC
3119 Gillham Road
Kansas City, MO 64109

Publisher: Jeremy D. Mohler
Editor-in-Chief: Alana Joli Abbott
Chief Operating Officer: Anton Kromoff
Senior Editor: Scott Colby

ISBN: 978-1-954255-71-5 (paperback), 978-1-954255-72-2 (ebook)
Worldwide Rights
Created in the United States of America

Translator: Giulia De Gasperi
Editor: Alana Joli Abbott
Galley Proofer: Em Palladino
Cover Illustration: Ann Marie Cochran
Cover & Interior Design: Jeremy D. Mohler

Printed and bound in the United States of America.

Visit outlandentertainment.com to see more, or follow us on our Facebook Page facebook.com/outlandentertainment/.

This work has been translated with the contribution of the Center for the book and reading of the Italian Ministry of Culture.

To my family and relatives:
thank you for your patience and support.
You truly are saints.

I

Anno Domini Invicti II

Turin, Tuesday, October 30th
St. Gerard, Bishop of Potenza

Despite the glass rattling, Sabino chose to turn the volume up a bit more. He wanted to feel the bass in his chest, not just in the air, a sensation that only true lovers of music could understand.

That morning he wore a blue baseball cap, back to front, and a loose hoodie with the letters "E.G." printed on the front. They were big, white, and they stood out. His jeans were hanging so low that it looked like they were about to drop at any minute, especially when, suddenly, he started to spin around.

Up since seven, breakfast Italian-style
pillow on my face and still hungover for a while
till yesterday my shithead neighbor told me:
"Turn down the music or I'll drown you in the sea!"

In his room, the bed wasn't made and his pajamas were on the floor in a ball, as if ready to toss in the laundry basket, even though they had been washed and ironed only the day before.

...Apulia on my cap
Turnips are my rap
Sea, sun, laughter
Hit me like a slap

Suddenly, the door burst open and Pia rushed in. As his uncle's perpetua—the woman who took care of the bishop's household—she'd been part of his life ever since he could remember. Now, she had her left fist on her hip, apron with an array of cooking stains and the "ladle of power" in the right hand—she wasn't in a joking mood.

Sabino almost didn't notice her. He was dancing, eyes closed, mesmerized by the notes and lyrics of the Bari Jungle Brothers, one of his favorite hip-hop bands. Walino, Torto, Ufo, Cyclone Tony, Max il Nano, and Preacher were his role models even though, unfortunately, he'd never had the chance to see them perform live.

When the music stopped abruptly, Sabino emerged from his state of hypnosis to find himself facing the rotating ladle. He immediately composed himself and looked down in religious silence.

"I have been calling you for the last fifteen minutes," the woman scolded. "But with all this racket, what else could I expect?"

Even though he felt embarrassed, Sabino tried to look at ease, moving his hand full of sparkling silver rings. "This isn't racket! This is *art*!"

"Lunch is ready. Art can wait," said Pia, leaving the room without another word.

Sabino gave up and followed her into the kitchen where he was immediately engulfed in the delicious aroma of baked pasta. His stomach rumbled, an echo of the hunger he'd earned dancing.

Pia had set the table for two with her usual care: the cutlery was wrapped in a linen napkin, and in the center sat a small vase with freshly cut daisies. The woman served him a generous portion of baked pasta. She was looking at him lovingly as a mother would.

"Where is Uncle?" Sabino asked, stabbing his fork into the piping hot pasta.

"He had a meeting. He is very busy today."

The boy's cell phone lit up as his ringtone sounded. It was rap music, again, visceral, angry, and most of all, deafening.

"Turn that thing off! We are eating!" yelled Pia, resuming her earlier harsh expression.

"Wait! It's Sharon! I have to answer it!"

The woman shook her head and poured herself some red wine while Sabino rushed to take the call.

"Hey, hi! I can't talk right now… What? Yes, everything is okay. The flight is at seven tonight. I'll call you back later, sweetie."

Sabino sighed. He couldn't wait to have her in his arms, caress her golden curls and breathe in her wild perfume, just like the heather found in the Scottish Highlands. Yes, once he was with her again, he would have the best Halloween of his life.

He did not turn off his phone, choosing instead to silence it. Pia seemed to have opted for the same, because she remained quiet for the rest of the meal. She did not say a word even when the boy started to clean his plate using a piece of bread, a habit of his she detested and tried with all her being to stop, without success.

After the baked pasta came the meat, then fruit, then a pie with sour cherries. The woman remained silent. Sabino watched her furtively, trying to figure out if he was the reason for her behavior. Guilt ate away at him and, giving up, he decided to speak.

"Okay, so, what did I do?"

"Who said anything to you?" replied the woman rhetorically.

"Exactly. You're not saying anything."

"Do you have a guilty conscience?" pressed Pia.

The boy did not reply but began instead to clear the table: an extraordinary event, considering that usually, after lunch, he would rush to the couch to watch tv. Unfortunately, his attempt was full of missteps. He first picked up all the crumbs, then he piled the plates, placing the smaller ones at the bottom and the bigger ones at the top. Then he quickly removed the tablecloth, letting the dirty cutlery fall to the floor. Pia shook her head, disappointed.

"Sit down," she said, in a serious tone.

Sabino wasn't sure how to interpret her request. Sometimes "sit down" could mean "you are going to listen to me now," so he obeyed her immediately.

"I am a bit worried about this trip of yours to London."

His tension dissipated, at least a bit, and he laughed.

"Come on! I'm not going to Australia!"

"True, but it is your very first plane ride."

Sabino raised an eyebrow. "My first plane ride? Are you kidding me? I was twelve years old the first time I flew!"

"I know," signed Pia. "I was with you when we all went to Nice on holidays. Of course, I was. But what I meant to say is that this is your first flight since our victory over the Luciferals. Will it be safe to fly to London?"

The Luciferals had been defeated the year before, and since then everything seemed under control. Sabino felt confident. However, the memory of that dark time full of fear and uncertainty about the future was still alive for many people.

"Absolutely! And if someone tries to be a dic—"

"Don't be vulgar!"

"Why not! My bros will take care of them! And then the Saints are here to protect us! We are in God's Kingdom! No one can hurt us anymore! *Hallelujah*!"

Pia smiled, and for a moment, the wrinkles around her eyes smoothed. "Your uncle would be happy to hear you talk this way," she said.

"I'll be gone only for Halloween, and then I'll be back. Don't stress about it!"

"Well, speaking of Halloween," said the woman. "I don't understand why people party in that pagan and tacky way! Everyone dresses up as monsters, carves pumpkins, and puts candles inside them… I shiver only thinking about it."

"Then don't think about it!" Sabino joked. "Don't worry! It's just a fun celebration and dates back to a very ancient tradition, if I am not mistaken. Just the other day, Sharon was telling me about its history."

When she heard that name again, a shadow swept over Pia's face. She then began to tidy up the kitchen, mumbling to herself.

"I need to call her back. Should I tell her you say hi? She's always asking about you."

It was then that Pia couldn't take it anymore; setting aside the tea towel, she continued to complain: "Of course, Sharon… Why couldn't you find a girl from here? Remember the saying: 'Stick to your own kind?' There is a lot of truth in it!"

They would regularly argue about this, and every time they would stall: Sabino would begin by teasing her, then he would get upset, and at the end he would tell her, quite emphatically, "We love each other!" adding, every so often, a more prosaic, "And she's gorgeous and all my friends envy me!"

They had met the summer before when Sharon came to Puglia on holidays with an older cousin. At the beginning, they would just look at each other and exchange half sentences. But eventually, things took the inevitable turn: they kissed on the beach, encouraging calls of seagulls in the background and a light breeze lifting Sharon's summer dress. Sabino had not turned eighteen yet; he did not know much about women—even though he pretended he did—and he had fallen hard for Sharon.

The first time apart had been traumatic, especially for Sabino. Sharon promised to write him every day, but he mourned immediately, barely eating for a whole week.

Uncle Alex suggested he find comfort praying. Pia told him, "Out of sight, out of mind," and his friend Gabry offered to introduce him to other girls, but their advice went unheeded.

"There are so many nice girls here, I really do not understand," Pia continued relentlessly. "For example, Mrs. Ranieri's niece, who goes to confession to your uncle—what is her name again? Annamaria, I believe. She is close in age to you and is always by herself. Why don't you ask her out?"

Sabino couldn't believe her words. "Are you out of your mind? Annamaria? She wears a retainer, and her taste in music is shi—"

"Stop swearing!"

"—terrible."

"Her features are lovely, and her eyes look like two stars. This is the most important thing. She will soon lose her retainer and her taste in music…" Pia waved her hands aimlessly, dismissing the idea. "Everyone has their own likes and dislikes! It is nice to widen your horizons, exchange ideas, talk about things."

"With her, I wouldn't be exchanging any ideas; we would just fight. Trust me."

"You are as stubborn as an ox," said Pia who, looking perturbed, resumed cleaning the kitchen.

Sabino went back to his room, turning on the stereo—keeping the music at a reasonable level this time—and jumped on the bed. He was still listening to the same band: the Bari Jungle Brothers:

Perhaps I have never told you, you look like a child,
You look like someone who doesn't remember the days gone by…

He grabbed his phone, going through his pictures and choosing one of Sharon, smiling, holding a bottle of Firkin, her blond hair in a ponytail.

He would finally see her that evening, after two months of texts and videocalls. He felt strange. He had never believed in the expression "butterflies in the stomach." What was swarming in his stomach felt more like a wasp nest. He wondered if it was excitement or anxiety—most likely both. The first feeling was normal, really, but why anxiety? He wasn't about to take a test. He had to call her, confirm his time of arrival, and say something nice. But he was procrastinating, keeping the rhythm with his foot while one of the songs of the Bari Jungle Brothers was playing.

He kept staring at her photo, thinking, when the screen lit up with her name. She was calling him. She had beaten him to it.

II

In the old attic, a thin drizzle streaked the gable's glass. The inlaid wooden chests, the faded carpets, and an impressive grandfather clock collection filled every corner, leaving very little room for Sabino, who was rummaging here and there. Between two wooden shelves, he noticed a very big spider web no one had thought to remove, as if its presence, in that place, was the most natural thing in the world.

Suddenly, a voice echoed in the room: "What are you looking for?"

The boy was startled and turned around immediately, nearly hitting his head on a rafter. "Pia! You scared me to death!"

He removed his baseball cap, running his hand through his hair to wipe the sweat, then he put it back on in his usual fashion, back to front.

"Come, give me a hand. I can never find anything up here, it's so full of sh—"

"Stop being vulgar!" Pia interrupted with a stern look on her face. "I can certainly help you, but first you need to tell me what you are looking for."

Sabino tried to open a drawer of an old dresser. It looked like it would be easy, but soon enough Sabino realized he needed to use both hands. He grabbed the handle, steadied himself on his feet, and after a minute of pulling and swearing, the drawer finally gave, moving a bit and raising a cloud of dust.

"What the f—"

Immediately Pia hit him on the head. "How many times do I have to say it? I do not want you to use such profane words. God, help him!"

"I can't find my vampire mask. I bought it a few years ago, do you remember? It should be here, somewhere. Where did Uncle Alex put it?"

"Oh, that one. Something to give you goosebumps. It was so horrible, in a bishop's house, of all places! Can you image what people would say? I might have tossed it."

"But what the he—heck are you saying, Pia?" answered the boy. "It wasn't on display in the parlor! And it is only a mask."

"Let me see," said the woman, opening boxes and moving aside objects strongly smelling of camphor. Finally, from the depths of a chest, she removed a dark ivory briefcase and a battered plastic envelope in the shape of a mask with long plastic teeth.

"Here it is! So disgusting!" she said, peeping into the envelope as if handling something infected.

"Give it to me," said Sabino.

"Hurry up now or you'll miss your flight."

Right then, the doorbell rang three times.

"Just a moment! I am coming!" shouted Pia.

Turning around she tripped on the briefcase, which had fallen onto the floor. It popped open, and she heaved a burdened sigh.

"Could you put things back, please?"

Not really up to it, the boy knelt. What looked like a cloth for mass stuck out of the briefcase. But the moths hadn't gotten to it. Strange for it to be here, in the attic.

"I'll take it downstairs," thought Sabino. "It can still be used. Uncle must have put it here by mistake."

He closed the briefcase, picking it up and bringing it downstairs, his mind following the rhythm of a hip-hop song. At the end of the stairs, he found an unusual scenario. Ten winged men, wearing sparkling protective armors, stood in an orderly fashion in the parlor, talking to Pia.

Sabino immediately stopped in his tracks to observe them: they were all blond, with light blue eyes and a sprinkle of freckles on the cheeks. Very difficult to tell them apart. There was no doubt. These men were Chrismatics.

"Oh my God!" Pia's shout brought Sabino back. He had been mesmerized looking at the men. "Of course, you can look," she said, more quietly. "We don't have anything to hide."

Sabino joined her while the winged men began to move around the house in a military formation.

"What happened?" whispered Sabino, biting his lips. "What do they want? Are you okay?" He tried to appear reassuring, but the heavy weight he felt on his heart made his voice wobbly and coarse.

Pia was pale, her hands shaking ever so lightly. She settled into an armchair in a corner and explained, weakly, "They arrested your uncle."

It took Sabino a few seconds to understand her words. They sounded foreign, almost unreal.

"It can't be! What the fuck are they thinking? But I—"

"Stop swearing!" Pia reproached him. "We should try to remain calm. It must be a mistake."

But Sabino was in no mood to remain calm. "Hey you, little angel!" said Sabino to one of the Chrismatics standing near Pia. "Hey, yes, you, I am talking to you. Where is my uncle?"

The man turned to look at him, spreading his majestic eagle wings. "If you are referring to Bishop Bafunno, he is at the cathedral, in front of Saint John." Then, looking up at the sky, he added: "May His grace shine forever!"

"You sons of b—" said Sabino, barely keeping his rage under control. He knew fighting was not going to be on an equal footing. "Pia, wait here. I am going to come back with Uncle Alex."

There was no time to waste. He turned around and made for the main entrance, overcome by a thousand doubts. He slammed into a silver armor.

"Fuck!" he swore, taking a step back. He quickly looked around. Every escape route was blocked. Who had sent them? And what did they want with his uncle? Fists clenched, he snarled like a tiger trapped by hunters.

The Chrismatic in front of him opened his wings, looking at Sabino sternly. "Stop! Before you can walk out of this door, we need to search you in the name of Saint John."

"I don't have time to waste with you, puppets!" protested Sabino. "I need to see my uncle! Move aside!"

Right away, Sabino felt both his arms trapped by two steel grips: two more winged beings had appeared next to him. The briefcase he was holding fell to the ground.

"Let me go! You, stupid puppets, let me go!"

His swearing was in vain. The warriors holding him seemed to have superhuman strength. Not matter how much he tried to free himself, they were keeping him still without any effort. The Chrismatic in front of him bent down to collect the briefcase.

"Leave it, goddammit!" shouted Sabino. "If you want to search me, do it, but do it fast!"

The winged man, unfazed, opened the briefcase. Suddenly, his expression brightened, just like the mosaics decorating the double-arched windows of cathedrals when hit by sun rays.

"Praise be to God," he said. "We found what we were looking for! Let's go back to the cathedral."

The boy stared at him with an incredulous look on his face: "You wanted the sheet? You could have just said so! Now, let me go. I need to go see my uncle!"

The Chrismatic threw the door open announcing, "Sabino Pignataro, you are under arrest for receiving stolen relics. Saint John will sentence you immediately." As soon as he finished speaking, he spread his wings and flew away.

"Me? Under arrest? Have you guys lost your mind?"

While Pia was crying, beating her chest and asking for forgiveness for the boy, Sabino found himself in midair, among clouds announcing rain. He tried to break free, despite the wind rustling his clothes. He moved his legs, searching for anything that could help him run. But as he looked down, his house became smaller and smaller until it finally disappeared. He felt sick to his stomach. His limbs began to feel numb and, in a flash, he lost his senses.

III

Unclear noises mixed with solemn hymns. A voice echoed in the distance, muffled.

"...a hearing, in the name of His Most Excellent Holiness Peter II Romano."

Sabino opened his eyes, suppressing the urge to throw up. Suddenly, an intense noise flooded his ears. Confused, he found himself looking down into the cathedral's piazza, full of people and lit by a diagonal light.

"Brothers and sisters, we are gathered here because of an unfortunate event."

The boy observed the crowd below him just like a tourist would from a tall building. He was overtaken by surprise and curiosity, and despite the ridiculousness of the situation, he smiled.

"Alessandro Bafunno, Bishop of the Most Holy Church of Dei Invicti Operae has committed horrendous crimes: he smuggled and received holy relics!"

Suddenly silence, as in a ritual, fell over the crowd. Sabino noticed that even the usual annoying drizzle had stopped. Only then did he realize how uncomfortable he felt: his hands and feet were tightly bound at the top of a pole under which there was a bonfire.

"What the fuck!" he shouted. "Get me down!"

The four Chrismatics watching him, each of them holding a torch, ignored his cries echoing through the silence of the piazza.

Bewildered, he realized that the crowd wanted to burn him alive, just like the worst of heretics. Grief and fear overwhelmed him. He felt a guillotine of terror on his neck; his silent cries of desperation wrapped around his bowels like painful stabbings.

"Monsignor Bafunno, what do you have to say in your defense?"

The authoritative voice belonged to a man in his thirties: tall, with flowing brown hair and a shaggy beard, his face bearing a haughty look. He wore a golden tunic; a fur coat was wrapped around his shoulders and the staff he held in his hand had a cross at its end. The warm light emanating from him instilled a strong reverential respect.

"Saint John," said a familiar voice behind the boy, "you know better than I do that one reaches the Kingdom of Heaven not with force but with faith and prayers."

"Uncle!" Sabino shouted as soon as he heard the unmistakable rhythm of his uncle's voice. They were tied to the same pole. "Tell him it is a mistake! Anyone can make a mistake, even the Saints!"

He sighed with relief. His uncle was okay and he would explain things.

"Are you perhaps trying to deny, Monsignor," John's voice silenced the boy, "that you sent a reproduction of the Holy Shroud to the Holy See and kept the original at your house?"

While the Saint was speaking, a Chrismatic handed him the briefcase that Pia had found in the attic. John opened it slowly, as if performing a ritual, taking out the sheet and unfolding it with a dramatic gesture.

"God of Adam, Noah, Abraham, and of all of us," he shouted, showing the sheet to the crowd, "show us your Power, hidden in this holy relic, so that your Will may be done and your Kingdom may come!"

"He is completely out of his mind, Uncle!" Sabino barked. "He is mistaking a simple sheet for the Holy Shroud! Ma vattìnne, va'—come on! It can't be!"

Suddenly, three tongues of fire, burning just like the Holy Spirit, appeared on the sheet. Cries of surprise and fear came from every corner of the piazza. Some people made the sign of the cross; others fell to their knees, and some others began to sing. Rivulets of blood coursed from the sheet, down John's arms, while the flames burned with vigor but never consumed the fabric. Even the Saint seemed to be engulfed in the fire burning around him. His mystical ecstasy remained unscathed.

The boy stared, mouth open, at that incredible wonder. There could be only one explanation: this was a miracle. In front of him stood the tangible proof that God fought by their side against the demons, and that, one day, thanks to the Saints, humanity would win.

Suddenly, as it started, the fire extinguished. John raised a hand mid-air and spoke to the crowd, who kept singing and praying.

"God has shown us his Power. Brothers and sisters, we are standing in front of the Holy Shroud the patriarch has been searching for months and that you, Alessandro Bafunno, hid in your home, even trying to deceive the Holy See. Are you going to deny all of this?"

The singing stopped, as if cut off by an invisible conductor, and in the piazza fell complete silence.

Sabino turned as much as his position allowed: "Uncle Alex?"

The bishop's look was resolute, but he did not say a word.

"Uncle Alex?" Sabino pressed. "He is wrong, isn't he? That isn't the sheet that was in the briefcase. They want to frame us, right?"

The man kept silent, as if he did not hear his nephew.

"Uncle! Say something! They are going to roast our asses!"

A black crow flew over their heads, landing on the pole, an ominous omen of death.

It was then that Bishop Bafunno spoke to the crowd: "People of Turin! The patriarch does not want the relics to worship them. He is only interested in their power! And his thirst for it will destroy us all!"

Those words stabbed Sabino's heart. With his eyes wide open and a shaking chin, the boy had to admit to himself that his uncle was truly a heretic. And soon, Sabino would be burned at the stake with him.

Then the bishop shouted, "Armageddon is near!"

The crow, cackling, landed on his shoulder, but the man paid it no attention.

"Uncle, have you lost your mind?" said Sabino, now close to exasperation. "Tell them we are innocent! Tell them you don't know anything about that damn sheet!"

"The witness has spoken," declared John with solemn composure. "He has admitted his sins and moreover he has pronounced blasphemous words."

"To the stake!" said vehemently a voice.

"He has to die!" echoed others in the piazza.

Sabino shouted and trashed about in an effort to free himself.

John nodded, and the Chrismatics walked toward the base of the bonfire with their torches.

"Fools!" said the bishop. "Armageddon will ruin us all! You need to protect the Holy Shroud! Save our souls!"

"Shut up!" threatened John, while everyone else shouted with fervor, as if they had all personally been mistreated by Bafunno and his nephew.

Using his eyes instead of his mouth, the Saint gave the order, and the Chrismatics set fire to the pyre. The crowd let out a cry so loud it was almost inhumane.

Sabino's survival instincts were stifled by guilt. His uncle had plotted against the Church. What kind of sick demon was hiding inside him, inside someone who had been such a paternal role model to him? How many souls had Uncle Alex corrupted without Sabino knowing? In the midst of his shame, a truth emerged from the depth of his subconscious: no matter the criminal acts his uncle had committed, why did he, his nephew, have to pay for something that didn't concern him?

His train of thought was interrupted by violent coughing, caused by the smoke. His eyes began to water and his throat burned like hell. Uncle Alex was also coughing, and the crow, thinking of the meal ahead, pecked here and there between clothes and cords.

"Alessandro Bafunno," said the Saint with a solemn voice, putting the sheet back in the briefcase, "you are found guilty of smuggling and receiving holy relics, and of heresy. Sabino Pignataro, you are found guilty before God of smuggling holy relics. God's people have expressed their sentence and I, John, son of Zechariah, protector of the city of Turin, confirm and execute such sentence."

Everyone present made the sign of the cross and replied: "Amen!"

"Amen?" was the only thing Sabino was able to say amidst his convulsions. "Fucking justice! I wasn't given the opportunity to speak! I am innoc—" A deep cough made it impossible for him to finish the sentence.

"Have faith, Sabino!" Bafunno told him, his face blackened by the smoke. But as he spoke, the man collapsed into a faint.

"Uncle Alex! Uncle! Answer me!"

Sabino's sight became foggy; smoke filled his lungs while the fire came closer and closer.

IV

Four gunshots echoed in the piazza. Immediately Sabino opened his eyes: he was in the air, next to his uncle. The Chrismatics who had taken part in setting the pyre on fire lay on the ground, like puppets with no guidance. White feathers floated upward, dancing in the air.

After a moment of silence that seemed like eternity, panic overtook the crowd. Everyone began to flee. From above, the scene looked like a river about to burst during the rainy season.

"Who dares challenge the Power of God?" thundered an irate John.

Instinctually, Sabino lifted his head. But what he saw made him sure he was still unconscious: he was dangling from the claws of a huge eagle heading, with difficulties, toward the tower next to the cathedral.

"Chrismatics, do us justice!"

Sabino looked below once again, taking deep breaths. Next to the pyre, there was now a woman, tall and slim, holding two smoking guns. She wore her red hair in several braids cascading over her very tight python-print clothes. Her eyes were hidden behind a big pair of sunglasses, giving her an even bigger aura of mystery.

Dozens of winged creatures took flight to gather around the woman, while others came together to form a wall encircling the fire.

Sabino's flight ended with a tumble, causing him to bang his face against the hard ground. Swearing silently, he noticed an unexpected change in the huge eagle. The wings closed, the feathers disappeared, and in front of the stupefied boy, the bird of prey transformed into a man with a strong build wearing a pinstriped suit, his hair pulled back into a ponytail.

"And who the fuck are you supposed to be?" Sabino slurred, beyond any possibility of politeness.

After fixing his tie, the man introduced himself: "My name is Ciccio. Take care of your uncle. I'll think about the rest. Lo capisti? Do you understand?" He had a very strong Sicilian accent.

Sabino wasn't sure he understood, but he did not dare say a word. He just nodded.

Ciccio studied him for a quick moment, then turned around with an ostentatious ease to face the Chrismatics; some were landing, getting ready to attack, but he didn't seem worried.

Sabino looked around, trying to count the enemies. In the center of the piazza, a fight was taking place between about twenty Chrismatics and the woman. She was so fast that by comparison, the winged men moved in slow motion. Her actions were elegant, effortless; she spun her red braids in a hypnotic dance. Many Chrismatics had already fallen to her infallible bullets. Still, they kept on coming.

In the meantime, a man with salt and pepper hair, wearing a camouflage uniform and an aviator brown leather jacket, appeared in front of Saint John. He pointed a big gun at the Saint's chest, at heart level.

"Your gun cannot do anything against my faith in God!" growled John, still emanating a golden light. His voice was so loud that it reached even Sabino. "Those who really believe are invincible!" he continued, lifting up high his staff with the cross.

"Uncle, Uncle!" Sabino, overwhelmed and afraid, began to shake the bishop, whose clothes were torn and burnt. "Dammit, open your eyes!"

Desperate, he turned around and saw that Ciccio had punched two Chrismatics: one was on the ground with a broken nose, and the other, next to him, had his neck twisted in an unnatural position.

"All good?" the huge guy asked Sabino, fixing his jacket.

"I'm okay," he said, though that was far from how he was feeling. "But my uncle doesn't want to wake up!"

It was then that Bishop Bafunno opened his eyes.

"I am taking you to a safe place, picciò!" shouted Ciccio, transforming again into an eagle. Sabino supposed if the Chrismatic-fighting shapeshifter wanted to call him a kid, he wouldn't object.

As they flew, they heard a gunshot. Sabino saw the aura around John become darker. Soon after, the man wearing the camouflage uniform fell to his knees, hit in the chest by his very own bullet.

The golden aura dissipated, and the Saint, crossing himself, said resolutely: "You are neither a human nor a demon. And you are no Saint either. But you are nonetheless a creature of God. May the Almighty receive you in his Mercy. Amen."

Suddenly, all went dark. The boy looked up and saw a huge, winged shape hiding the moon. Among the cries of the crowd, the enormous being swooped down into the piazza, shaking the ground violently as it landed.

The immense creature was terrifying. The majority of the

Chrismatics had been smooshed under its four clawed feet, and its two snake-like heads, placed on both ends of the long, bat-winged body, were feasting on the victims. Its jaws opened wide, letting out a simultaneous growl, and its pupilless white eyes sparked intensely.

The woman with the red braids fired dozens of bullets at it, with no result. The empty loaders fell to the ground in a metallic clunk. She looked unfazed, her black glasses reflecting the monster biting two Chrismatics.

The sight of the beast terrified Sabino. As soon as his feet touched the ground and the eagle took flight again, he turned around to cast a desperate look at his uncle. He felt dizzy.

It was impossible to run away.

"Stop, hellish creature!" shouted John, closing his eyes, engulfed in the golden light once again. In one hand he held the briefcase with the Holy Shroud, and with the other he lifted the staff with the cross into the air.

"God is with me! There is nothing you can do against His power!"

The beast turned sideways, and both its heads sped toward him. When the fangs of the monster shattered against the dome of light surrounding the Saint, a growl full of anger and pain echoed across the piazza.

"My name is John, son of Zechariah, protector of this city, and I reject you in God's name. Turn back to the abyss!"

The two heads convulsed. The wings and the scaly body jolted, and dark smoke poured out of its glassy eyes.

A sudden gust of wind caused the Saint to fall and lose hold of the briefcase with the Holy Shroud. The case vanished across the piazza, before it reappeared, hanging from the claws of a majestic eagle in flight.

A wing of the huge beast struck John, catapulting him against the main door of the cathedral. One of the two heads tried to swallow the eagle while the other exhaled a foul greenish vapor that completely engulfed the bird.

Sabino winced when he saw the eagle hit the tower, falling miserably next to his uncle. As it crashed, the bird transformed back into the man with the pinstriped suit who had saved them: he had fainted and was now covered in a burning green substance. Not far, the briefcase with the Holy Shroud was almost completely corroded.

He wanted to help, run away, do anything—but his body kept on shaking. So, he looked at the blank stare of the unholy beast that seemed to be aiming in their direction.

A cry died in his throat before coming out: even his vocal cords felt immobilized.

"You…son of a bitch!" The voice belonged to the man wearing the camouflage uniform, now back on his feet, standing next to them. Breathing heavily and drenched in sweat, he looked like he had just woken up from a nightmare. He retrieved his huge gun and checked his chest: his injury was gone. What was left was only the hole in his leather jacket. The boy stood open-mouthed: how was it possible that camo-guy was still alive?

"Watch out!" Sabino shouted.

Warned, the man fell to the ground and rolled over, barely missing a lethal claw from the monster.

"Hey!" he shouted back at Sabino, getting up immediately. "Are you okay?"

His thick foreign accent reminded Sabino vaguely of Sharon's.

Getting more and more confused by the minute, Sabino gave him the thumb up. The guy was really weird: he had a hole in his chest, a huge paw had almost flattened him, but his first thought had been that of asking a complete stranger how he was doing? Who the heck was he? Why did he care?

Sabino's thoughts crashed to a halt: The monster had taken notice of the guy and was aiming at him with one of its heads, getting ready to attack. In the meantime, the woman with the red braids had realized that her partner was back on his feet.

"Egil! You're alive! God be praised! Let's send this beast back to Hell!"

"You got it," he replied. "Let's rock and roll!"

His hand wrapped tightly around the pendant he was wearing—a cross with a dragon—and he focused. A crimson sparkle appeared, becoming bigger and bigger until it engulfed his entire body.

One head lunged forward, opening its jaws. They snapped shut on the man with such force that the noise of broken bones echoed in every corner of the piazza. The beast began shaking its head violently, while from its mouth poured out a slimy green liquid; a spear with a dragon wrapped around it was stuck between its jaws. It belonged to camo-guy, who was now wearing a shining knight's armor.

The three spaulders, the armbands, and the greaves all displayed an array of spurs. The chest was decorated with a Latin cross, around which a dragon was coiled. He wore a red cape bearing the same image.

Sabino breathlessly admired the man in armor. He was more

powerful than the Wagnerian Siegfried Pia always talked to him about, and more charismatic than the medieval knights on the album covers of the metal bands his friend Gabry liked so much. But the main difference was that those were fiction, while this one was real and was standing right in front of him.

On the other side, the second head of the monster stabbed downward to bite the woman who, like lighting, jumped on top of it and began running down its neck, firing round after round. Chilling growls of pain came from both heads of the beast.

"You like Argentum, right?" she shouted. "Don't worry, I have plenty more."

The knight, following her example, jumped on the other head and pierced its muzzle from side to side with his spear.

Suddenly, the monster jumped, spreading its wings and sending the woman plummeting off. She tumbled to a gentle landing, bending her knees.

An ominous glow lit the cathedral, and from the throats of the monster came a cloud of green vapors and fumes that enveloped the two, then spread to every corner of the piazza. Sabino gagged, deafened by the roaring thunders. As he turned from the scene, he realized his uncle was lying still on the ground. He rushed to him, terrified.

"Uncle, are you okay?"

The bishop turned around very slowly, as if each movement required superhuman effort.

"Sabino…" His voice was like a whisper, his breathing heavy, his eyes dull. "Sabino, save the Holy Shroud."

"Of course," replied the boy, almost choking. "But I need you to be okay!"

"No… No! Save it!" Coughs wracked the bishop's chest. "The Martyrs…"

He did not manage to finish the sentence. He slumped back, fainted. Sabino wanted nothing more than to stay at Uncle Alex's side, but he forced himself to respect his uncle's wishes. Sabino ran to collect the briefcase, keeping an eye on the monster's movements. The knight with the shining armor was on his feet once again, despite his serious injuries. The cut on his chest began to glow, emitting a red light. He spread his arms; behind him appeared a big Latin cross as he lifted the spear with the dragon coiled around it and hurled it into the sky, where Sabino lost sight of it among the clouds.

The cross disappeared from behind the knight's shoulders, only to appear on the monster's body while the spear plummeted toward the ground. The clouds opened up, ripped apart by the spear. The weapon crashed into the monster, which fell in the piazza, destroying the pavement and demolishing two nearby buildings.

The man removed his helmet and carried his fainted friend in the pinstriped suit on his shoulders. Stumbling, he walked toward Sabino, who had returned to his uncle's side, clutching the briefcase. The pyre's fire had almost died out. The boy ran to meet the knight, afraid. "We need to call for help! My uncle is dying!"

"No one can escape God's judgment!" said an imperious voice.

The boy spun: even though he was burnt and wounded, John was standing there in front of them. With a cross, he reached out to touch the forehead of the knight, who seemed petrified.

Sabino shook, mumbling words that had no meaning. He had thought the Saint was gone, but he had underestimated him…

"Evil always turns against itself," said John, "while God's glory is big. You are fools and murderers; your lust for power is bound to crush you."

The boy was confused. But he remembered vividly his uncle's instructions: save the Holy Shroud. He tightly squeezed the briefcase, wondering what he was supposed to do with it.

"Blasphemous heretics like you deserve the eternal torments of Hell!" denounced the Saint. "I have decided to be indulgent. I will let you die with your sins washed away, so that if God is willing you will go to Heaven."

Sabino looked to the knight for help, but despite his own supernatural abilities, the knight stood, still petrified.

I wonder if my uncle wanted to give the Holy Shroud to these people, thought Sabino. *But who the hell are they? It is true that I would be dead by now if not for them, but still…*

"Sabino…" John called his name, sweetly but firmly, as if talking to a child. "You still have time to repent. Give me the Holy Shroud and you will be forgiven."

The knight's eyes narrowed, just slightly, with determination to fight, and Sabino realized that he was petrified against his will, not out of fear. Suddenly, all Sabino's doubts vanished. He knew what he had to do.

"Go fuck yourself, boomer!" he shouted with a rage deeper than he'd ever known. "If you want the sheet, come and get it!"

And, with these words said, he began to run.

"God's mercy is great toward those who repent, but His wrath is infinite for those who are proud!" thundered the Saint.

The golden aura surrounding John intensified. He closed his eyes and prayed, "God, make me an instrument of your justice! Receive the souls of these poor sinners."

Sabino turned around, as if to bid Uncle Alex one last farewell. He saw the bishop there, close to dying, next to where the man in the pinstriped suit, the woman with the red braids, and the armored knight now stood. He thought of their heroic acts, and in an instant, he made his decision: he could not abandon them. He couldn't let other people die for him.

"Stop!" he shouted, coming back. "This is all my fault! Let them go!"

"Rejoice, you all!" said John. "God welcomed my prayers! Soon you will be forgiven! Holy waters of the Jordan River sweep away the sinners and give them eternal rest!"

An imposing column of clear water shot up from the center of the piazza, growing higher and higher toward the sky. With a deafening roar, the liquid wave crashed to the ground, pulverizing the surrounding buildings.

"Behold God's power!" shouted the Saint, now suspended in a golden sphere, sixty feet above the ground.

The boy felt useless: he'd failed in preventing a catastrophe. He looked again at his uncle, the man in the pinstriped suit, the knight, and the woman. He gently put down the briefcase and opened his arms wide in front of the terrible flood that was about to hit them. Silently, he asked them all for forgiveness.

The first sputters of water hit him hard. He shouted as loudly as he could, and his cap flew away. An explosion of light invaded the piazza while a dove descended from the sky.

In a place beyond time,
in an infinite instant.

The light was blinding, and Sabino tried to shade his eyes with his hands. As if by magic, a human-like figure appeared. It was majestic, three-winged, perhaps an angel or something very similar. His face, framed by long, smooth, white hair, had blurred, indistinct features that conveyed all the same an image of beauty, of symmetrical perfection.

"Listen to me, Sabino." His voice was melodious, and at the same time, disturbing. "God's grace is now with you, new Martyr! God loves you all, and he would want to see you united in His name! Go and save the world!"

In a cacophony of wings, hundreds of doves took flight, and before he could realize it, Sabino felt the earth open beneath his feet and plunged in the deepest darkness.

"Have faith!" The angel's voice sounded distant, muffled, as the boy continued to fall into the void. "Faith is the Martyrs' strength, and it will bring you closer to God."

The wind lashed his body; his heart raced and his hands searched frantically for something to hold on to.

He let out a sharp, loud, desperate cry, an extreme plea for help. And then he was gone.

V

Most Holy Capital of the Kingdom of God on Earth

Wednesday, October 31st
St. Quentin, Martyr of Vermand

His Most Excellent Holiness Peter II Romano makes His entrance in the Sistine Chapel!"

Arael tapped his staff three times on the floor, and the heavy carved doors opened with a loud creak. He would finally have the chance to closely admire their savior. He hoped his eyes did not betray the curiosity eating away at him.

After a time that seemed infinite, a boy about fifteen years old entered the room, walking with long and rhythmic steps. He was all dressed in white. He had a golden tiara in his blond hair, and in his right hand, he held a long staff displaying a crucifix on top. To Arael, the boy's eyes seemed to show naivete, a certain kind of pure innocence. The other Chrismatics present knelt as he walked past them, lifting their wings high as a sign of devotion.

The boy, with solemn composure, approached the imposing golden throne, lined in red, at the center of the frescoed hall. Above it hung a Latin cross within the Star of David, the symbol of Dei Invicti Operae Church.

Two men knelt on either side of the throne. The one on the left had olive skin, the appearance of a young Greek philosopher, and luxurious purple bishop's clothing. The one on the right looked more like a stereotypical friar: robust, white skin, tonsure. Under his arm, he held a very heavy looking book.

Peter II Romano took his seat on the throne while silence ruled over the hall. Behind him loomed the fresco depicting the Last Judgment. A ray of sun shone on the raised right arm of Christ, the Judge, making the painting even brighter.

"His Most Excellent Holiness Peter II Romano holds an extraordinary audience!"

When Arael pronounced the official formula he had been taught, everyone stood.

"The Holy John, protector of the city of Turin, makes His entrance!"

The other herald, standing opposite the other end of the door, tapped his staff twice and the doors re-opened. All the Chrismatics knelt again, but this time they did not lift their wings.

The Saint entered the hall, casting not a single glance at the guards. Steadfast, he quickly reached the throne, immediately kneeling before the young leader: "Forgive me, Your Most Excellent Holiness. I felt the urgent need to speak to you."

"Get up, John," ordered the boy patriarch, the expression on his face neither sad nor preoccupied. "We were worried about you, as bad news reached us from the city of Turin. I sensed the appearance of dark powers, and for a moment, I feared the worst."

"Your Most Excellent Holiness," John said, his voice thick with awe, "God's power is great! I witnessed it in Turin!" His eyes were filled with ecstasy and wonder.

"John," Peter II Romano interrupted him, "the latest events must have been upsetting to you. Take a moment and clear your thoughts. And the rest of you, leave us alone!"

The winged men bowed and left, as orderly as soldiers.

Arael and the other guard, as per official protocol, remained in the room, silent.

"So, John," said the patriarch in a serious tone, "you can confide in me. Open your heart to God and tell us what happened to you."

"Today, God's grace has lit up all of Turin," the Saint began. "As Your Most Excellent Holiness suspected, Bishop Bafunno was hiding the Holy Shroud in his house with the help of his nephew."

Arael's surprise reverberated through his wings. He immediately tried to assume an unperturbed expression, just like the other Chrismatic. Arael's veneration for the patriarch prevented him from looking away; at the same time, he could not show interest in the conversation taking place in front of him.

"Not only did he hide the holy relic," pressed Peter II Romano, "but he was also a member of a heretical sect. Am I right, Thomas?"

"Yes, you are correct," answered the plump white man with the habit, leafing through his bulky volume. "During their search in his house, the Chrismatics found some compromising letters in which the bishop claimed to belong to a sect known as the Hand of God."

As soon as Thomas pronounced those words, Augustine, the man dressed in red, gasped. "Those heretics!" he shouted angrily. "They are the most painful thorns on the side of the Holy Church of Dei Invicti Operae! As if the curse of the Luciferals wasn't enough!"

"Calm down, Augustine." The soothing voice of the patriarch seemed to come from another dimension. "Thanks to God's power and to the sacrifice of men of good will, we were able to contain the menace of the Luciferals. People have resumed their lives under the guidance of His Almighty."

"Your Holiness," resumed Augustine, still angry, "for centuries people longed for tangible signs of God's Presence, and now that they are here, nothing has changed: people still err."

"But as of today, everything will change!" said John, full of emotions. "Today, like hundreds of years ago, my eyes witnessed the power of the Almighty. The Messiah has returned to us!"

"What do you mean?" asked the patriarch leaning forward, his voice cracked by apprehension.

"Three unknown heralds announced him, defeating a horrible hellish creature." An expression of joy spread across the Saint's bearded face. "The waters of the River Jordan touched him and the dove of the Holy Spirit descended on him... Everything was light!"

The smooth traits of Peter II Romano's face twisted in anger. "Holy Spirit? Don't be blasphemous! Don't you understand what huge risk we took? Give the Holy Shroud to Augustine, immediately!"

"Your Most Excellent Holiness," John's voice became somber, "the Holy Shroud wrapped itself around the Lamb of God when he manifested himself to all of us!"

"No!" said the patriarch with a suddenly loud voice. "No! You betrayed our Lord! You can no longer differentiate between what is true and what is false!"

The young patriarch was surrounded by six pairs of fiery wings, as a blinding light spread through the chapel. Arael used his wings to protect his face while an unbearable heat filled the air.

"This, John, is the power of God! Emerge from the darkness of your mistake and behold your *true* Light!"

Thomas and Augustine knelt, crossing themselves.

"Your Most Excellent Holiness," replied John still standing up, "just as I recognized the Lamb of God during the reign of Herod, so I recognized him this time. I am certain of it. I am not mistaken."

"John the Baptist, you have fallen victim of the false illusions of the Devil. I relieve you from your duty as protector of the city. Augustine, I want him locked in the cell of atonement where, I hope, he will soon find his sanity."

The man wearing episcopal clothes bowed, accepting the order by saying, "Fiat voluntas tua."

He grabbed John by an arm and led him toward the door.

"He who showed himself to me is far more powerful than you, Your Most Excellent Holiness," said the Saint, while Augustine opened the door. "We are not worthy to untie His shoelaces."

With a muffled sound, the door closed, and silence returned to the hall. Arael felt a shiver run down his back.

Peter II Romano asked Thomas, "What else do we know about Bishop Bafunno?"

The friar fixed his tonsure with one hand. "Your Most Excellent Holiness, some of the letters found in his house were addressed to Bishop Boenzi of Padua. It seems he is also affiliated with the Hand of God."

"Lord have mercy on him," said the patriarch with a sigh. "Who else is mentioned in these letters?"

"No one in particular, Your Most Excellent Holiness," replied Thomas, leafing through his volume.

The Chrismatic on the other side of the door tapped his staff twice, sending an echo of the dry and sharp sound through the hall. "Saint Augustine is now entering the room!"

The red-robed man reentered at a solicitous pace. In front of the throne, he knelt. "Your Most Excellent Holiness, my soul is deeply troubled. What could have happened that was so serious to make Saint John lose his mind?"

Peter II Romano stood abruptly, causing Augustine to crane his neck to gaze up at the young patriarch. "He still witnessed a crucial event, despite being confused by the Devil. The terrible signs he saw can only have one explanation."

With these words, he strode from the throne, walking to the small and simple altar in front of Michelangelo's fresco. The two Saints followed him, respectfully and keeping their distance.

The patriarch made the sign of the cross: "Thomas, my son, I need to ask you to set aside your love for the contemplative silence. I urge you to finish telling me what you have discovered in Turin."

Thomas shut the book and replied, "The only other thing worthy of your attention is the discovery, in the bishop's home, of a very old papyrus in Aramaic. I did not have the time to analyze it, but I believe it is part of the Gospel of Joseph of Arimathea."

"The worst heresies come from the apocryphal Gospels, Your Most Excellent Holiness," interjected Augustine.

"I understand." The young patriarch knelt and closed his eyes to pray. "Lord, enlighten my mind. Show me your Will."

Suddenly, the wall burst into blue flames. The frescoed figures began to move, chanting hymns to the Lord. They were all singing the same song, some in Latin, others in Greek, and still others in Aramaic. Thomas and Augustine, visibly amazed, knelt in front of the miracle. Arael's wings fluttered again. He had not believed it was possible to admire the patriarch any more than he already did. But he was wrong.

Then, Patriarch Peter II Romano opened his eyes again. The flames, gone. The figures, in their places. One could only hear a faint Latin litany in the distance, fading away.

"There is no doubt," he said. "Judgment Day is near. What John witnessed has only one meaning: the Anti-Christ is among us."

Thomas and Augustine made the sign of the cross several times. Arael couldn't refrain from casting a terrified glance to the other winged guard. The other Chrismatic also had lost his indifference.

"He will do everything in his power to tempt us," resumed the patriarch. "He misled John by pretending to be the Lamb of God in order to take the Holy Shroud. The Devil sent him to weaken us and to undermine the foundation of our faith."

"This will never happen!" blurted out Augustine. "Your Most Excellent Holiness, the Devil will never be able to corrupt those who are pure of heart!"

"It is true what you say," Thomas added quietly. "However,

if even Saint John, who is the example of faith for all of us, was confused by the dark power…"

"My sons, calm down." The clear voice of the patriarch had the effect of immediately soothing the agitated souls. "Being in turmoil only strengthens the power of the Devil, whose aim is to divide us. I advise you not to share the news: God's pure lambs would panic. Let's limit the damages," he said looking directly at Arael. He then sat back in his throne, placing his hands in his lap as if waiting for something. The Christmatic felt as if bathing in the purest of light.

"Fiat voluntas tua," replied Augustine and Thomas.

The voice of Peter II Romano echoed louder in the hall. "Good. Hard times are coming, but I am confident that we will win over Evil. Thomas, you are in charge of looking into the so-called Gospel found in Turin. I feel it is going to be useful to us in preventing the moves of the Anti-Christ."

"I will start right away," said the Saint.

"We trust you," added the patriarch. Then, to Augustine: "I would like you to question John. We need to find out every single detail on the Anti-Christ, his 'heralds' and his ties with the Bishop of Turin."

"As you wish, Your Most Excellent Holiness."

"Tell the diocese of Padua. Put Bishop Boenzi under surveillance. Use discretion. Get ready, Augustine. As soon as the Anti-Christ shows him again, you need to find and fight him."

"I am ready, Your Most Excellent Holiness. My heart beats with the desire to erase God's enemies."

Arael nodded. He was also ready to do whatever it took to make sure Good prevailed.

"Go now, and bring me back good news. I will stay here and pray God."

The two Saints left. Before joining them, Arael, his soul still full of light, stood for a moment, studying the patriarch all alone in the empty hall. Arael had been wrong. In his light blue eyes there wasn't naivete.

There was a stormy sea.

VI

Padua

Sabino opened his eyes, still feeling stunned. He looked around, his breathing labored, his heart racing. He was lying down in the back seat of a big car. He could hear the unmistakable rumble of its motor and those of the other cars driving by.

His head rested on the knees of the woman with the red braids and dark glasses. He recognized her right away, even though he did not know her name.

"What is..." he tried to ask, realizing he was having a hard time because he was exhausted. "What is your name?"

"Shhh," she replied, stroking his hair. "Just rest now. You are safe."

Her voice was warm and comforting. The boy did only what he could. He closed his eyes and enjoyed this sublime moment of peace.

"Amunìnne, picciò! Come on, kid! Wake up! Wake up!"

He startled awake. Ciccio was unceremoniously slapping his face. He did not know how long he had slept. They were now in a rest area.

"Boss, avàst!" he protested, getting up. He shoved his way out of the car—a metallic blue sedan—before getting another slap.

Still half asleep, he saw the woman with the red braids walking toward him: she was balancing a tray with four steaming plastic cups.

"Ah, you woke up!" she said. "Do you want a coffee?"

"Sure, thank you," answered Sabino.

He took one of the cups, at the same time looking his savior up and down.

She looked like a femme fatale. She was in her thirties, and her tight clothes highlighted her fit body. On her right-hand ring finger, she wore a flashy silver ring with an eye enclosed in a triangle.

He realized he'd stared at her for far too long. He was attracted to her, and that made him uncomfortable. He tried to get out of it and took a sip from his cup.

"Shit!"

The coffee was too hot and almost burned his lip.

"We bent over backward to save you. The least you can do is try not to hurt yourself," joked the woman, smiling.

The boy felt so ashamed, he wished the earth would swallow him then and there.

"I am Arian, by the way."

"Nice to meet you!" he replied. He tried to shake her hand, forgetting the cup, which fell to the ground almost staining the woman's dress.

Arian shook her head and walked toward the others.

"This is Egil," she said giving a coffee to the man wearing the leather jacket and the camouflage pants.

"Hi!"

Sabino studied him. He clearly went to the gym; he had a strong jaw line and looked like he was in his forties, if only because anyone younger would have known better than to wear that style of mirrored glasses.

The usual fanatic, Sabino thought, noticing that the guy was wearing a Latin cross shaped pendant with a dragon coiled around it.

"You already know my name, picciò!" Ciccio slapped the boy so hard on the shoulder he almost chocked.

Ciccio, wearing his elegant pinstriped suit, stood next to Egil. On his left wrist he sported a solid golden bracelet engraved with a wolf's head. It didn't suit him at all, just like his strong Sicilian accent. He drank his coffee in one go and then lit a cigarette.

"Well?" blurted out Ciccio, slapping him again. "Are you going to tell us your name or not?"

The boy, surprised, replied, "Oh, sorry… Right… My name is Sabino, but my friends called me DJ S.P."

"Come on boys!" Egil said abruptly. "Enough chit-chatting! The Chrismatics are closing on us. Let's go!"

The other two nodded.

"Just a moment," said Sabino, making sure he had everything. "My cap. It must have fallen in the car."

As he reached up, as though he could feel for the cap on his head, he noticed a white bandana with red stains wrapped around his left forearm. "What is this supposed to be?"

"Do not take it off!" Arian ordered in a firm tone. "Under any circumstances!"

"What do you mean? Is this a joke?"

"Not at all," said the woman with a stern look on her face. "Forget your cap. You must have lost it in Turin."

"In Turin? Why? Where are we now?"

Egil closed the doors of the sedan, locking it behind them, and explained quickly: "We're in Padua. But stop asking questions! They're looking for us, and we don't have time to waste. Let's try to be inconspicuous, okay?"

He turned and walked away, followed by Arian and Ciccio, who had to put out his cigarette before he'd had the chance to finish it.

"Wait…but…how is my uncle?" asked Sabino, rushing to join them. "Did they catch him?" His heart was racing.

Ciccio waited for him to catch up and said in a low voice, "Your uncle is at the hospital. Now that they've seen us, they are going to squeeze him like a lemon to obtain information. But he needed medical attention, and we couldn't take him with us. Don't worry, he will be okay. But you have to be quiet now!"

The boy nodded and followed the others through the narrow streets of what looked like the city center. Padua was still waking up. The traffic lights were just switching from flashing yellow to their normal setting. An inviting aroma of coffee and freshly baked croissants wafted out of the cafés. The traffic noise was barely audible, and luckily no Chrismatics were in sight. The four arrived in front of a white stone, three story building. A regal-looking marble lion's head peered at them from the lintel in the majestic wooden door.

A prolonged beep came from one of Sabino's pockets. Egil, Ciccio and Arian turned around, casting an annoyed look at him.

Sabino, embarrassed, took out his phone. He saw several missed calls from Sharon and a message: "Where are you? I am incazzatissima—so, so pissed off!" He smiled. Sharon loved swearing in Italian.

"What's going on?" asked Egil.

"Nothing, just a friend," replied Sabino trying to sound unfazed. "Excuse me, please. I have to make a call."

Ciccio, swiftly as a bird of prey, grabbed his phone: "Are you joking? It could be traced. You can't use it anymore, lo capisti? I think it is better if I keep it."

Sabino tried to fight back, thinking how Sharon was never going to forgive him. Ciccio, however, could not be persuaded.

While Egil knocked on the door, the boy noticed, on the left, a huge marble stone, with an inscription in one of those dead languages he could not stand.

Arian moved beside him. "Do you want to know what it says? It is a tombstone in honor of the sacrifice made by the citizens of the city on January 8, Anno Domini Invicti I."

"I don't quite remember," said Sabino, "but I am sure it refers to one of the carnages committed by the Luciferals."

"Yes, exactly," confirmed the woman. "The Cathedral of Saint Anthony was attacked by a mob. No one was able to stop them, and many among the military and the general population died, until..."

Creaking on its old hinges, the door opened just enough to allow the nose of a white-haired woman to cautiously squeezed out. Her eyes, light blue and alert, inspected the dim light.

"Yes?"

"We belong to the brotherhood in medio est virtus," replied Arian. "Bishop Boenzi is expecting us."

"I know nothing of this," said the woman bitterly. "But do come in and take a seat. I will check the calendar."

After a few minutes in the waiting room, the four were ushered in the private study of the bishop, a short man with a round face and a curly tonsure. He had small but laughing eyes.

"Please, come in, my friends," he welcomed them.

The room was big, rectangular in shape, with a soft chestnut-colored carpet covering the floor. In front of the door was a big desk where many books lay open, while behind it, on the wall, there was a beautiful crucifix, standing almost five feet tall. The side walls were covered with shelves full of religious volumes. Sabino smiled. The smell of old books and their arrangement reminded him of his uncle's studio. For a moment, he felt at home.

"Thank you, Marta," the bishop said to the older woman. "You may go now. Remember that I am unavailable until tonight."

With a slight bow, the housekeeper left the room.

"Nice to meet you, Bishop Boenzi," began Arian.

"Welcome," replied the man, considering the group as though he wanted to study them. He rummaged through the shelves, looking for something, and moving the volumes in the front with clumsy and erratic gestures. "There is a book I want to show you..."

Sabino did not have much time to ponder about the book because, suddenly, a whole section of books slid backward and downward to reveal a narrow passage. The bishop turned to look at them with a big smile, then gestured for them to follow him.

The passageway descended several feet underground, lit here and there by luminescent stones that gave the walls a vermillion, almost sinister, appearance.

Sabino's nerves made his voice unsure. "Ciccio? We are safe, right?"

"Minchia, picciò. Wow!" answered the other, giving him one of his slaps. "Muto devi stare…you really need to shut up. You'll have all the answers soon."

"All right, all right," said Sabino, huffing. Ciccio was treating him like a little boy, and despite his apprehension, he was getting tired of it.

After a few minutes, they reached a pitch-black cave. As soon as the bishop set foot in it, big flames appeared in suspended braziers. Sabino jerked back. He still wasn't used to these wonders.

In the center of the cave stood a big black table surrounded by five leather chairs. The flames made the shadows dance, deforming them in a macabre way.

"Please, take a seat," urged the bishop, sitting as well. "I was waiting for you. We can speak freely here. I would first like to know your names."

"Ermenegildo Bertolini," said Egil taking a seat, "but perhaps Egil will sound more familiar."

The bishop stared straight ahead, as if trying to find some important information in the back of his mind. Just a flash, a mere instant.

He took a gun out of his pocket and shot Egil in the forehead. Surprise appeared on Egil's face, while two streaks of blood trickled down from his eyes.

"Holy fuck!" said Sabino, frozen by fear.

Another flash and two guns were pointing at Boenzi's head: Ciccio and Arian weren't in the mood for joking.

"Stop!"

Egil's voice echoed in the cave. He wiped his face using a handkerchief and gave the bullet back to the Bishop, grinning as if he had played that part at least a dozen times before. His forehead was as good as new.

"So?" he asked calmly, "do you trust us now?"

"Divine Martyr, please, forgive me!" whispered the bishop, rushing to his feet. "We have very little time, and the Chrismatics are watching me. I needed to be sure that..."

Sabino was speechless. He picked up the bullet off the table and looked at it carefully: it was a real one! His weak certainties vanished for the very last time. His head was spinning.

"Please, forgive me," Boenzi repeated. "You can never be too careful these days. So, you are Egil, the Martyr consubstantiated with Saint George's sacred relics."

"Exactly," said the man showing the pendant shaped as a cross with the dragon.

"It is beautiful!" said the bishop with admiration.

"My name is Marianna Luisetti, and I welcomed the holy spirit of Saint Lucy," said Arian, showing her silver ring with the eye within the triangle.

Ciccio lit a cigarette, uncovering his solid gold bracelet with the wolf's head. "And I am Ciccio; I belong to the Corleone family. I share this body with Saint Francis… Do you mind if I smoke, ah?" A grayish smoke escaped from his mouth, its smell making Arian wrinkle her nose in disgust.

"Lord's Glory is great!" said the bishop. "How I wish all my predecessors could witness this event. But please, tell me, have any of you had the privilege of coming in communion with the Holy Shroud?"

Egil, Arian, and Ciccio immediately turned to Sabino.

"What is wrong with you?" Sabino demanded, getting more confused by the minute. "What the heck? This is not making any sense! And my uncle…"

"Speak respectfully!" Ciccio slapped him again. "It is true this is a cave, but we are still in a church, lo capisti?"

"Enough!" Sabino stood up. "Two days, two days these absurd things have been happening: the Holy Shroud in my uncle's house, the fire, the two-headed monster, you three making miracles happen, the apparition of the angel or whatever that was with the long hair—"

"An angel appeared to you?" the bishop interrupted. "And what did he say?"

"Something like 'You are a Martyr,' and 'Have faith.' I've tripped before but nothing like this! Could you tell me what kind of a mess I'm in? And why am I not supposed to take this white bandana off? How is my uncle? How is this going to end?"

Sabino broke off, panting from having gotten caught up in his speech.

"Do not worry, Sabino Pignataro," Bishop Boenzi reassured him. "Sit down and you'll know everything there is to know."

"How do you know my name?" asked Sabino. "I have never seen you before!"

The bishop shook his head and, with a smile full of good-natured compassion, said to the boy, "Well, since you escaped the fire, you have become famous among the journalists. And the Chrismatics are looking for you..."

"Bastards!" exclaimed Sabino. "But how is my uncle?"

"Alessandro and I are very good friends," continued Boenzi. "He is still in the hospital, in critical condition."

"I want to speak to the doctors! Ciccio, give me my phone back!"

"Better not," said Arian, placing a gentle hand on his arm. "Trust us. No one should hear from you, at least for now."

"Your uncle told me so much about you," said Boenzi, "and you are exactly as he has described you: stubborn and a non-believer. But he loves you a lot and has always said that one day, you'll use your potential to achieve something big."

Sabino could feel his nose starting to pinch and his eyes watering. He stood still, with his head in his hands, trying hard not to cry. In the cave, there was only silence and the smoke from Ciccio's cigarette wafting slowly toward the ceiling.

"Okay, man," said Egil, "let's hurry up! We have little time."

"All right," replied the bishop, putting his hand on Sabino's shoulder. "Your uncle and I belong to a very, very old brotherhood founded almost two thousand years ago by the followers of Joseph of Arimathea. Do you know who I am talking about?"

Sabino lifted his head slowly: "No, I don't know. Who would this Joseph be? The father of Jesus?"

"Not at all," interjected Arian. "Joseph of Arimathea, according to the Gospel of Luke, was one of the few members of the synedrion who opposed Jesus's sentence. According to Matthew, after Jesus' crucifixion, it was Joseph, together with Nicodemus, who buried our Teacher."

"Well done, young lady!" said a very pleased bishop. "Your explanation is precise and thorough."

"So?" Sabino demanded. "Why did they put my uncle and me on the pyre?"

"Joseph of Arimathea," continued the bishop, "was the thirteenth disciple of Jesus; he had an important role in the Jewish community, so he could never reveal that he was a 'subversive.' But, thanks to his status, he was able to obtain permission from Pontius Pilate to bury our Teacher. When he rose, Jesus gave the Holy Shroud and the cup containing his divine blood to Joseph to keep until the moment…"

"Hey, just wait a minute," interrupted Sabino, "are you talking about the Grail?"

"Yes, the Holy Grail."

"Okay, I understand…and so?"

"Joseph and his disciples kept the Holy Shroud and the Grail save for centuries, as his Gospel tells us."

"But aren't the Gospels by Matthew, Mark, Luke, and John?"

"Those are the Gospels that the Church of Dei Invicti Operae consider 'valid.' There are others considered apocryphal—like the Gospel by Joseph of Arimathea, for example," explained Arian.

Boenzi continued, "Since we are Joseph's disciples, we have passed on his Gospel from generation to generation, without sharing it with others, as he wanted."

"So, my uncle," whispered Sabino, "is a disciple of Joseph of Arimathea?"

"I'll tell you even more. Your uncle and I, together with other three people, are the last disciples left. Under the guidance of Bishop Grassano of Bari, we divided Joseph's sacred scriptures among us and gave ourselves a name."

"The Hand of God," concluded Ciccio, putting his cigarette out. "Is everything clear now, picciò?"

The new information dizzied Sabino. "But at least I know now that my uncle really tricked the patriarch and kept the Holy Shroud at home," he sputtered. "Wow, we almost got roasted!"

"Joseph's Gospel," said the bishop, "says that one day, thanks to the relics, Jesus will be reborn to save us all."

"So why not give the Holy Shroud and the Grail to the patriarch?" asked Sabino. "He is the voice of God on earth! He brought the Saints back to life and he saved humankind from the Luciferals!"

"There are a few things you don't know," the bishop said with a sigh. "Peter II's ambition has no limits—may God get rid of him! As soon as his army of Saints is ready, he will cause Armageddon!"

Sabino shook his head. "Armawhat?"

"Armageddon is Judgment Day in Hebrew," explained Arian.

"That is why he wants more and more relics," continued Bishop Boenzi. "When he decides he is strong enough, he will kill the remaining Luciferals and vanquish humanity."

"But this is crazy!" Sabino protested, frowning. "Have you all gone mad? Why would the patriarch want to wipe us out?"

"Why, do you ask?" The bishop's expression became stern. "Why did God send the Flood? Why did he make fire and brimstone fall on Sodom and Gomorrah? Why?"

Everyone remained silent, waiting for the answer to all those life or death questions.

"Because we are sinners!" Boenzi told them. "We complain, we are mean, we are human. And our flaws, even though they are natural flaws, displease His Most Excellent Holiness. Armageddon would be the beginning of a new, perfect era, where only Saints and Chrismatics would live, following God's laws. Do you understand now? If we were to give the Holy Shroud and the Grail to Peter II, it would be our end."

"If this is the way things are, then…" Sabino shook his head, fear clawing at his stomach. "Holy shit, we are fucked!"

"No," said Boenzi. "God is great, and in His infinite love, He has showed us a way."

"So, you have a plan?" Sabino asked, grasping for hope. "What is it?"

"We put all our hopes on the Martyrs, as we call them," explained the bishop, pointing at Sabino's three saviors. "For reasons unknown to us, some holy relics have become part of them. Bishop Grassano trained them, and now they know how to control the holy spirit of the Saint within them to perform real miracles. I believe you have seen them in action, no?"

"Mmm... Yes, I have," Sabino confirmed, "but they will never succeed. It is just three of them against all the patriarch's Saints and Chrismatics."

Ciccio lit another cigarette and said, "I wanted to punch all of those blond puppets in the face, but unfortunately things got complicated."

"Yup," Arian agreed. "In Turin we should have come into communion with the Holy Shroud, following the instructions of Digitus Minimus."

"Digitus Minimus," Sabino asked.

"Your uncle, Bishop Bafunno," Arian explained.

"Things did not go that way," said Egil. "Luckily Grassano advised us to come and talk to you if need be. Anyway, the communion with the Holy Shroud did happen... What do you say, Sabino?"

Memories of the fire, of his dying uncle, of the scary wave, of the light, the dove, the angel formed in Sabino's mind... He felt sucked into a vortex, but he tried hard to remember what had happened.

Then, all of a sudden, he understood. His eyes fell on the bandana around his left forearm.

"It can't be..." he whispered, more to himself than to the others.

"Praise to God!" exclaimed the bishop, moving closer to see the relic. "It is the consubstantiated Holy Shroud!"

"Consubwhat?" asked a stupefied Sabino.

Arian smiled at him. "We call consubstantiation the miracle that allows a relic to become one with the body of a person, transferring to them the faculties of the saint it belonged to."

"But tell me, Sabino, what happened?" asked the bishop, curious. "How did the miracle happen? If we could unveil this mystery..."

Arian had become agitated. "I don't mean to interrupt, but I have a very bad feeling."

"Minchia! Shit!" exclaimed Ciccio, unwillingly putting out his cigarette. "Your Excellency, you now know everything. Tell us what to do before it is too late."

"He who is now one with the Holy Shroud," explained Boenzi, "needs to do the same with the Holy Grail to reach Apotheosis and avoid Armageddon."

"Who? Him?" asked the three Martyrs at the same time.

"Me?" followed Sabino who couldn't believe his ears.

"Yes, you," replied the bishop, walking toward a rock wall. "The Shroud did not choose you by chance, Sabino. You must have faith!"

"Picciò, lo capisti?" repeated Ciccio, giving him a slap on the shoulder. "You must have faith!"

Mixed voices came from above, together with the sound of quick footsteps.

"Holy fuck!" exclaimed Sabino. "They found us!"

The bishop firmly pushed a slightly protruding rock. The surprised Martyrs witnessed the rising of a big portion of the rock wall that unveiled another dark and secret passage.

"You are not safe, even here! Quick, go!" the bishop urged them. "I will hold up anyone coming. Reach the convent of Cascia. Tell them you are sent by Digitus Secundus and ask to speak with

Abbess Cinzia, Digitus Medius. She might be able to tell you where the Holy Grail is."

"All right, but where does this tunnel lead?" asked Egil.

"It is an escape route, built centuries ago," explained the Bishop. As a big rock closed the entrance to the passage, he added, "Follow the rising sun and you'll be safe. Be quick!"

With a loud noise, the big rock closed the passage, and the four Martyrs found themselves engulfed in total darkness.

"Follow me!" urged Arian. "We need to hurry!"

The darkness wasn't very pleasant, but to Sabino the idea of being left alone there was even worse. Who knew what kind of strange beasts lurked among those tunnels? Better to follow the Martyrs; he plucked up courage and joined them in the darkness.

VII

The cold light of their flashlights ripped through darkness that ended at a compact rock wall.

"This is the end of the line!" announced Arian, touching it in a vain search for an opening. "We can't go any farther. This passage also is a dead end."

"That sucks!" shouted Sabino bumping for the umpteenth time against Ciccio who, arms crossed, was staring, disappointed, at the insurmountable obstacle. "When are we getting out of this shithole? It's pitch black and smells bad."

"We've been circling around for more than an hour," Egil pointed out, sounding worried. "We can't waste any more time."

"Shut up!" ordered Ciccio. "Listen."

The darkness seemed to be whispering—a distant, rhythmic, and melancholic call. Sabino had a sudden fear of ending up eaten by terrible mermaids hiding in the shadows, singing captivating songs to lure them into their traps.

"Am I mistaken, or do I hear an organ?" asked Ciccio.

"Yes," Egil confirmed, pointing to the ceiling. "And also, the sun is shining on our heads."

They pointed their flashlights upward to illuminate some marble slaps covering a lower section of the passage. One was decorated with a worn-out high relief that was still recognizable: the sun coming up behind the mountains.

After a few seconds of hesitation, Arian pondered: "Rising sun… marble slabs…organ. There must be a building above us, maybe the cathedral." She bit her lip. "Something doesn't feel right…"

"Minchia," complained Ciccio, who was clearly impatient. "Let's try to find a way to get out of this prison…I can't take it anymore. I can't breathe." He ran a finger inside his shirt's sweaty collar.

"Keep calm." Egil clapped a reassuring hand on Ciccio's shoulder. "We'll find a solution, don't you worry. Arian, let's go back and try the right passage."

Once again, the beams of light searched the darkness. But as Sabino followed Arian and Egil, grunts and growls sounded from behind him. He glanced back, where Ciccio stood, shaking.

"Egil?" said Sabino. "I think Ciccio's not feeling well…"

"Come here, quick!" shouted Arian, grabbing his arm and pulling him to her.

He stumbled behind her, confused. He watched over Arian's shoulder as hair sprouted all over Ciccio's dark shape, and his body surged height. All the while, his groans and gurgling sounds continued. In the flashlight's shaky light, Sabino saw Ciccio's muscles spasming and clothes ripping apart; sharp fangs gleamed in the darkness under two bloody eyes.

The humongous hairy creature hurled his fists up high, punching into the roof of the tunnel. The ground shook. In a rain of dusty rumbles, the ceiling collapsed while the organ music kept on playing. Light filled the passage where a huge, angry gorilla kept on growing.

Suddenly, the music stopped; the mighty primate leaped out of the tunnel. Looking up, Sabino recognized the Cathedral of Saint Anthony, where, in its center, now stood the colossal gorilla, so tall that its head almost touched the ceiling.

The terrifying beast pounded his chest with his fists a few times; his growls were so powerful that the church's crystalline windows shattered. Sabino noticed a crowd of worshippers flee in a complete panic, trying to avoid the rain of shards.

"Damn!" exclaimed Egil, leaping out of the huge opening, immediately followed by the other two. "Just our luck!"

They were in a beautiful lateral chapel.

"Come on, let's try to save this place from Ciccio's fury," Arian urged Egil, drawing her guns.

Sabino was still taking in the scene when a group of Chrismatics approached the primate.

"Devil's beast, leave this sacred place!" they ordered.

The gorilla grabbed two of them, neither much bigger than his hand, and threw them against the precious marble wall. Dozens of spears pierced the animal, but the beast, seemingly unharmed, walked toward the central nave, absently stomping on some of the Chrismatics; others were left agonizing by his powerful punches, and some others were buried by the collapsing rubble of the chapel's torn lintel.

Sabino kept a safe distance, watching from behind a pew as Arian and Egil approached the unstoppable gorilla.

"Ciccio, can you hear me?" asked the knight, once again wearing his armor and brandishing his spear. "Come to your senses! We need to leave this place!"

"Stay back!" Arian shouted to the Chrismatics, holding them at gunpoint.

Sabino blinked. He couldn't make sense of Ciccio's transformation.

Was that big hairy beast really him? Why was he acting so irrationally? The music coming from the organ had not stopped; instead it was getting louder and louder. The gothic cacophony seemed like the perfect soundtrack.

Suddenly, the giant ape turned toward the main altar. His muscles, almost spasming, relaxed, and his expression became calmer, nearly serene. Following the creature's focus, everyone turned to look in the same direction. The beast had stopped growling, and only the music from the organ could be heard.

In the center of the nave, a figure wearing a gray friar's habit and a hood pulled up over his head walked slowly, holding a blond baby in his arms. A warm light, getting brighter and brighter as they advanced, enveloped them.

Egil lowered his spear, Arian holstered her guns, and the Chrismatics knelt. Time stood still. Even the gorilla knelt in front of the friar while the baby stretched his arms toward his snout. Sabino lowered his head as a sign of respect, a gesture that surprised him, even though totally spontaneous. The friar put the baby down and the infant began to crawl toward the beast. The ape lowered his head until it touched the floor, closing his eyes, while the delicate hand of the baby grazed his huge nostrils.

"Grande é o poder de Deus—God's power is great," said the friar finally, throwing back his hood.

He had the stern look of the righteous man who had witnessed every type of obscenity and atrocious act; his voice was firm but warm, like that of a loving father. Addressing the group, he scolded, "You, adoradores de demonio! You, Devil-worshippers! How dare you desecrate this holy place? I, Fernando Martins de Bulhoes, who entered the graça de Deus as Anthony, protector of the city of Padua, will put an end to your arrogant insolence."

"Son of a…" hissed Sabino; he wanted to react but couldn't budge as he was profoundly under the spell of the baby.

I must have faith, he thought, trying very hard to convince himself. *Uncle and Boenzi said that those who have faith prevail…and so can I!*

As he tried to fight the profound feeling of awe that entrapped him, he was joined by the friar. With a blessing demeanor, Anthony addressed him: "Você não me engana Anti-Christ!"

Of the entire sentence, Sabino understood only the last word; he'd never been good at Portuguese.

"Anti-Christ? What are you saying? We are the good ones!" he wanted to reply. Instead, the presence of the baby tied his vocal cords.

"Your Spirit, from the outside, looks like the one from Our Lord, but I can tell good from evil," Anthony continued. Then pointing to the baby, he shouted: "Behold the splendor of the true Deus!"

Sabino saw the baby play on the gorilla's shoulder: with his tiny hand he caressed the creature's hairy cheek and, in return, the beast squinted his eyes and tilted his big head toward the child while his sharp jaws turned into a faint smile.

"Entende?" continued Anthony, satisfied. "Your lethal beast cannot do anything against the power de Deus. Your appearance não me engana, inimigo; I am not fooled by enemies of the faith!"

Sabino was confused. He stared a bit longer at the small creature, thinking how much the child looked like the images of Baby Jesus he had seen in churches and in his books.

"Gee…That can't be," he thought. "If the baby is really Him… we…we must be on the wrong side…"

"Anti-Christ! Traidor!" Anthony accused. "Now you will die by the hands of your own servants."

With light and rhythmic steps and sporting an inquisitive look, the friar walked up to Arian. "Sinful and immoral mulher, I give you the opportunity de redimerti—repent! Rise up against the Lord of deceits and your pecados will be forgiven."

In a blink of an eye, two guns aimed straight at the Saint's forehead.

"Goodbye," said the woman, scornfully pulling both triggers.

Instead of two bullets, the barrels released two white lilies.

"May the Holy Lily purifica teu espírito," replied the Saint, walking away.

While his sandals smacked the floor of the cathedral, Arian was showered by petals until she was fully covered. From above, the purest water fell, dissolving her body until only a bouquet of lilies and her two guns were left on the expensive marble.

"Amém, amen!" added Anthony crossing himself without turning around.

Sabino felt his heart tightening. He didn't know what to think anymore: until an hour ago, he was sure he'd been on the side of good, but now, suddenly, everything looked like a tragic mistake. Warm tears ran down his cheeks, and he fell to his knees, his head bent down.

"Lágrimas de crocodilo, você está condenados," Anthony rebuked; Sabino didn't understand all of it, but he knew the Saint thought his tears were false, and that the friar considered him condemned. "I did try to save you, but there is no hope for you de redenção."

The friar walked to Egil, who was still staring at the baby, and began to place lilies in the openings of his armor.

"May the Holy Lily purificar teu espírito," said Anthony.

The lilies grew, blossoming into a huge tree, as a ray of light descended through the chapel's ruined roof. On its branches, the knight's armor swung, wrapped in roots and leaves.

"Amém, amen!"

The Saint made the sign of the cross and finished his prayer. Then he turned to Sabino: "Anti-Christ, traidor, the souls of your followers are now purified of sins and are joining Deus. What remains now is the soul of this poor beast, corrupted by your blasphemy."

He took a few steps toward the gorilla, stretched his arms in front of him, palms open, and recited: "Lethal beast, free yourself from this blasphemous bond! Break your chains and do justice on your mendacious master in name of the Almighty!"

The child with blond curls laughed happily, caressing the gorilla's snout. The animal responded to the child's smile with closed eyes and an expression of pure beatitude.

"Are you ignoring the chance offered by the Almighty?" the friar threatened. "Very well then. Holy Lily, purify seu espírito!"

From above, a cone of light swept over the gorilla and the baby. A drop of the purest water fell, ever so slowly. It landed on the baby's hand, turning into a lily, which he offered to the gorilla.

"Impossìvel!" exclaimed the friar, bewildered.

Before his eyes, the baby was offering the flower to a man, no longer a horrible beast, barefoot, wearing a threadbare brown habit, whose smile conveyed a sense of deep calm.

Anthony gasped, squinting his eyes and shaking his head. "You are not going to corrupt me using the false visage of our master Francis! I will not tolerate any more blasphemy in my cathedral!"

Sabino's tears had dried; he was too confused by the scene unfolding to grieve his own fate. With a solemn gesture, the Saint brought his right hand closer to his forehead.

"Your corrupted Spirit does not deserve the purity of the Holy Lily," he said in a somber, almost cavernous voice.

Anthony placed his hand by his heart.

"You'll have a taste of the sofrimentos you will suffer on Judgment Day."

A mystical golden light enveloped Anthony, making him glow with grace. He stretched out his right arm, and from his hand appeared a tangle of thorny, burning branches, protruding toward Sabino's kneeling form.

My end is here... Sabino thought as the thorny flames darted toward him. *I hope God will forgive me.*

From above, a huge hairy hand grabbed the thorny bramble. Ciccio's palm, burnt and wounded, pulled the branch away from its path. His grip did not loosen as the flames raged, but instead got tighter.

"Temeroso," said Anthony, "your attempt is futile! Nothing can save your master!"

The bramble, forced to stop, thrashed convulsively in the gorilla's grip. With a terrifying growl, the beast yanked the burning branches. The friar, still holding on, launched from the ground and crashed into a column. It shattered into a thousand scattered pieces.

Sabino noticed with dismay that in the beautiful, frescoed apse, the crucifix was crying tears of blood.

The shattered column began to glow, so brightly that the intensity became blinding. When Sabino finally opened his eyes, he saw that the brambles had been replaced by a wreath of white lilies. In the middle of it stood Anthony, looking unscathed, without a scratch, even though his habit was ruined in several spots.

"Você nunca ganhará—you will never win," the Saint declared. "The enemies of the Almighty have no chance of vitória."

Sabino's body relaxed, no longer held as firmly in the veneration that had frozen him. He glanced at the baby, who was frowning, looking almost sad.

"Die, murderous beast!"

From the Saint's palms sprouted more thorny, burning branches, aiming them at the gorilla's neck.

"Holy Burning Bramble! Burn the body of this creature and purify seo espírito!"

He tugged at the brambles and, despite the size difference, was able to lift the beast, throwing him to the marble floor. The gorilla spat blood, pierced by the thorns and burned by the fire; he thrashed around with all the strength he had left.

The baby crawled toward Sabino, wide eyes at the brink of tears, and stretched open his small arms. Sabino picked him up and stroked his curly little head.

Amid the gorilla's screams, the flames rose high in an explosion of heat. Then silence.

"Amèm, amen," finished the friar making the sign of the cross.

Sabino shuddered. His eyes were dried from too much crying; he realized he was alone. If even the baby had come to him for protection, what could Sabino possibly do against the righteous fury of a Saint? But more importantly, was it the right thing to stand against divine punishment?

A column of incense-scented smoke rose from the floor where the remains of the dried-up brambles lay, mixed with ashes.

Anthony turned toward the boy and, seeing that Sabino was holding the crying baby, had a moment of hesitation.

"This is your last trick," he finally said, with regained control. "You are not going to fool me."

The baby hugged Sabino tighter and tighter, sobbing. The child's blue eyes stared at him and seemed to beg for salvation.

"You are wrong, little one," Sabino whispered, trying to loosen the baby's arms from his neck. "There is nothing I can do to help you."

"Get ready to suffer, Anti-Christ," the Saint threatened Sabino. "Your time has come! Holy Burning Bramble, purify seu espírito and vanquish his false illusions!"

Golden flames lapped branches of brambles that darted from his hands. The moment seemed to expand endlessly. Sabino stared into the baby's clear eyes. He could hear the child's little heartbeat in his ears and feel the warmth of that tiny body clinging to him, seeking protection. He couldn't accept that such an innocent and defenseless creature could suffer because of him. He could never forgive himself.

Even with his legs shaking, he stood, with the baby still clinging to him. He stretched out an arm, hand open, palm facing the brambles hurling toward him.

As in a dream, the brambles stopped their course, and Sabino's white bandana radiated a warm light.

Suddenly, the green vines fell, shriveling, to the floor, where they caught on fire. From it, a phoenix with golden feathers took flight, landing with a shriek on the cathedral's rooftop. Then, with a swift turn, the phoenix swooped toward Anthony, extending its sharp claws. It was Ciccio! He had transformed once again!

The flames died down, and Sabino stroked the head of the baby who stopped crying.

"Im…pos…sìvel… im…possi…ble," stammered the friar. "Tal um grande poder! Such a great power!"

At that moment, the bird of prey came back with a screech; Anthony dodged the attack by throwing himself to the side. The bird glided on the marble floor and transformed, slowly, into the barefoot friar, wearing a ragged brown habit, who had appeared to him earlier.

"Anti-Christ traidor!" Anthony shouted. "Stop pretending to be Francis! Stop it!"

But the command went unheeded; a green aura enveloped the brown-clad friar, his bare feet turned into pawing hoofs; a tail flowed out of the habit, growing from an equine rump. In no time, the humble friar had turned into a unicorn with an ebony coat.

"Holy Burning Bramble," prayed Anthony, nervousness making his voice waver, his palms outstretched, "sweep away these false apparitions!"

As a new tangle of thorns sprouted to life, the unicorn lowered its horned head and galloped at full speed toward the Saint. Hundreds of glowing needles pierced the unicorn's flesh; it neighed in pain but continued its race at full speed until it reached its opponent.

Pierced in the chest by the animal's horn, the Saint finally collapsed, his limp form shuddering still against the unicorn's mighty head. The creature stopped for a moment, as if to catch his breath, then shook his head, shrugging off the friar's body.

The baby had resumed crying and screaming; Sabino bounced the child in his arms, trying to calm him down. In the meantime, a pool of bloody tears had formed under the big crucifix in the apse, now streaked with red rivulets.

The crackling of a match diverted the boy's attention from that terrible sight. Ciccio stood next to him, lighting another cigarette. His pinstriped suit was ripped in several spots.

"Come on," said the man, touching the fallen friar with his foot. "You have enough little flowers. Give me back my friends, lo capisti?"

"Teacher Francis," said Anthony, "me perdoe. I did not recognize you."

"Don't 'teacher' me!" replied Ciccio, exhaling smoke. "You turned my friends into lilies. Make them humans again!"

"I swear, I just wanted to fight evil in the name of His Most Excellent Holiness," retorted the Saint, his deep wound weeping blood. "I have always had the honor of talking to the Almighty... and now that my time has come, I can't hear His voice any longer."

The baby squirmed in Sabino's arms; the young man lowered the child to the ground. Crawling, the baby wiped away his tears and approached the friar to strike the Saint's head with his little hand.

"Gloria in excelsis Deo, I hear the voice of the Almighty again..." He grabbed Ciccio's hand, reaching up from the ground despite his pain. "Teacher, your pupil was wrong and now, about to die, he humbly asks for your forgiveness. Você pode me perdoa—will you forgive me?"

Ciccio met the eyes of the curly-haired child.

"Okay," he replied, crushing the cigarette stub under the tip of his shoes. "I forgive you."

"Obrigado, Teacher." The features of Anthony's face relaxed. "Muito obrigado."

The baby placed his small hand on Anthony's chest. As soon as the child touched his wound, a blinding light filled the entire cathedral. The outlines of the room's features melted in that absolute glow.

When, after an unquantifiable period of time, the light softened, Sabino saw the friar standing with the child in his arms. On his left stood Egil, wearing a necklace of white lilies; on the right, Arian, wearing the same.

The Saint made a gesture of farewell and walked toward the majestic crucifix. The Martyrs turned their backs to him and left through the main entrance, the only architectural element still defined within that sea of white.

Sabino thought he was being called. He stopped to look back. The child, in Anthony's arms, waved his small hand. Sabino smiled.

The crucifix was no longer crying.

VIII

Padua's Highway Tollbooth

The red and white striped bar lowered behind the blue sedan, which immediately zoomed into the acceleration lane.

"Hold this, please," said Egil, driving, giving the ticket to Ciccio in the passenger seat.

"Minchia," Ciccio cursed impatiently. "Hold on to it yourself. Don't you see that I am busy?" He was trying to tighten a bandage around his left arm, using his teeth.

"You would be a great embalmer," teased Arian from the back seat.

She turned to Sabino, looking to share the joke, only to realize that he was staring, stunned, at the landscape outside the window. His eyes were wide open, his nose was pressed against the glass, and he was biting his lips: he seemed to be stuck in a cage of worries.

With a gesture now normal to her, Arian arched her left eyebrow and found herself in the shapeless space of the boy's conscience. A bloody crucifix, shrouded in burning brambles, stood against a very white horizon. Black smoke filled her nostrils. From the clouds of soot emerged a unicorn with a dark mane who, coming toward her, repeated: "Will I make it? What is the right thing to do?"

"Don't wait for other people to answer your questions."

Her sudden response shattered the silence in the car. She coughed, then turned, as if nothing had happened, to watch the trees at the side of the road from behind her glasses.

"Were you talking to me?" asked Sabino.

"Rather, find the answer within yourself," she added, still looking outside her window.

"But…How do you know that…"

"Please, Arian," joked Egil, "don't you see that the Anti-Christ has a crush on you? Leave him alone."

"A crush? Me?" Sabino sputtered. "What the fuck are you saying?"

"Watch your language, picciò," said Ciccio. "She can read your mind. No point in denying it."

Arian's mind was once again assailed by Sabino's relentless conscience. Even though the boy was trying to think about something else, she could clearly feel his subconscious urges; they were everything but innocent. It was a wasted effort.

"Don't worry, I am used to it," she reassured him.

"No…You know…" Sabino tried to reply, shaking and rambling. "Actually, I don't…"

"Never mind," Arian sighed. "Why don't you tell us a bit about yourself instead? With everything that has happened, we haven't had the time to talk."

"Good idea!" agreed the former military man, who was accelerating to pass a truck. "Tell us about you, your parents…"

"Yeah, come on! I really want to have a good laugh." Ciccio leaned back in his seat to light a cigarette.

Sabino remained silent. For what seemed like an interminable moment, they could only hear the speeding cars and the humming of the motor.

"What is it, picciò? Have you lost your tongue? Or is the smoke bothering you?"

"To tell you the truth…I never met my parents."

Ciccio began to cough convulsively, letting out puffs of smoke.

"Great job guys," said Arian. "Great job indeed."

"Sorry, man," apologize Egil, slowing down a bit. "If it is going to make you feel better, no one in this car has had an easy life."

"It's all right. Uncle Alex and his family always made me feel at home, in Bari and in Turin."

"I am sorry," commented Ciccio, "I was a real—"

"It's no problem," Sabino cut him off, embarrassed. "Other than that, I love rap. One day, DJ S.P. will rock the world!"

"Tell me—" Arian's voice had a tint of mischief. "Do you have a girlfriend?"

"I don't really…"

"Don't lie."

Sabino cleared his throat. "I meant, I don't really expect questions like that…but yes, I do have a girlfriend."

"Did you hear that, Egil?" Ciccio began to shove his elbow into his companion's arm. "He has a girlfriend! And what is the name of this carusa, if you please?"

"Sharon," explained Sabino, staring into Arian's dark glasses, trying in vain to catch any sort of emotion. But nothing.

"Is she from the States?" speculated the former military man.

"No, she lives in London. She was waiting for me last night. We were going to spend Halloween together. That reminds me…I need to call her. Ciccio, give me my phone back."

"We got rid of it, amico," Egil said, looking at Sabino in the rearview mirror.

Sabino glowered. "Are you crazy? And how am I supposed to get in touch with Sharon now?"

"Picciò, you are not going to contact anyone." Ciccio took a final drag from his finished cigarette. "As soon as you make a phone call, the Chrismastics will be upon us. All the phones are tapped, lo capisti?"

Sabino lowered his head, resigned.

"So, her name is Sharon and she lives in London…" prompted Arian. "Tell us more."

"What to say…" Sabino drummed his fingers on his knee. "She lives in Greenwich but her parents are Italian…"

A bitter smile appeared on the woman's lips. "What a strange coincidence…"

"What do you mean?" Sabino's brows furrowed as he looked for clues behind her dark glasses.

"I also knew a Sharon, with Italian parents, who grew up in Greenwich," Arian explained. "She worked with me at the General Archives of the Most Holy Capital of the Kingdom of God."

"No, my girlfriend is a freshman in college," explained the boy. Then, mellifluously, he added, "Did you say the General Archives? Congrats! As far as I know only geniuses get hired to work there."

Arian leaned back in the seat, her posture almost bored. "I have a degree in Ancient Letters and another one in Cultural Heritage Protection, with a specialization in Archival Studies, that I earned while working in what was once known as the Carabinieri Corps."

"Really? Wow! Two degrees! How old are you?"

Her eyebrow quirked up above her glasses. "You should know that you are never supposed to ask a woman her age."

"I meant to say," Sabino tried to explain, "that you look too young to have two degrees already. Oh well, forget about it. So, you were talking about your colleague, Sharon..."

"I wouldn't press the subject," suggested Egil.

An awkward silence followed.

"Sabino is now one of us. I think it is better that he knows the story," said Arian finally, her tone resolute. "Sharon and I worked together on translating and cataloging ancient tests written in Aramaic. She was brilliant, and together we produced precise work. But one day, something changed..."

The woman pushed her dark glasses a little higher up her nose.

"Two papyri were found near the Dead Sea. One was given to me and the other one to Sharon. From the start of the project, Sharon stopped collaborating with me. Then she began to avoid me entirely, as if we were two total strangers. Worse, my presence bothered her so much that she moved into another office."

"No wonder," said Ciccio, winking at Sabino. "Can you image working with *you* every day? If only I could also move to another office!"

The woman ignored him and continued. "Moreover, the text given to me was in very poor condition and had quite a few references to the other text. To understand it, I needed to read the text given to Sharon. She had hidden it somewhere and refused to show it to me, even though I tried to convince her that working together would benefit us both."

She was quiet for a bit. That part of the story seemed to make her feel nervous. Egil pumped the brakes, almost in sympathy with the pause in the story, but Sabino realized that other cars were slowing down on the road around them.

"Let's hope it is not an accident," huffed Egil.

"And then what happened?" Sabino prompted Arian to continue.

She resumed reluctantly. "One day I decided to go for it. I wanted to find out where she was keeping the papyrus. Unnoticed, I followed her and discovered that she had access to the underground tunnels of the Archives, where some of the most important and precious treasures of antiquity are kept."

"Really?"

"Yes. Papyri, scrolls, paintings…even some holy relics. And while I marveled at all those wonders—"

She broke off, becoming stiff.

"Arian?" Sabino prodded.

"Enemies on the roof!" she shouted, and a terrible thud followed. The car's tires skidded to the left, out of control, and two huge, clawed paws tore through the roof like it was tissue paper. Sabino landed on Arian's chest. She had taken out her guns with incredible speed but had failed to fire them.

A big lion head poked through the opening in the roof, roaring, and pointed straight at Egil.

The maniac driver grinned. "Let's rock!"

Egil regained control of the car, counter steering it to the right and slamming down on the accelerator. Everyone in the car was thrown to the left, terrible lion included—the beast clamped its jaws just above Egil's head.

As soon as he felt the heavy breath of the lion on him, Egil counter steered again and somehow took out his huge gun. He pointed it straight into the lion's mouth and fired.

"Buon appetito!"

The impact forced the lion's head out of the car. Taking advantage of the moment, Egil turned around once again and pulled the hand break. His maneuvers spun the car around several times, knocking the animal off the roof.

Finally, the car stopped in the middle of the lane, while other cars sped past, honking madly.

The lion landed about thirty feet ahead. Its coat was as white as milk, and it had eagle wings that made it look even more proud and determined. Riding it was a man with olive skin, black curly hair, and a thick beard, proudly displaying his sumptuous purple robes. Arian recognized him immediately. It was Saint Augustine.

He raised his crosier and solemnly announced: "Punishment is justice for the unjust! Anti-Christ deceiver, surrender to the power of God! Hand over the Shroud and abandon your evil intentions!"

Arian pulled herself up out of the car, rising to her feet with feline grace on the torn roof.

"Go!" she shouted to Egil, aiming at the opponent's head.

When she fired, the beast spread its wings, and the bullets bounced on the feathers like rubber balls.

"Do you refuse God's forgiveness then? I, Augustine, son of Patrick, doctor of grace by the Will of the Almighty, will end your nefarious deeds!"

The sedan skidded past the lion and sped on. The animal took flight and set off in pursuit of the car. Arian did not miss a single shot, but every one of them bounced off the skin or the wings of the lion, which protected the Saint with its body. Passing two cars on the right, the sedan entered a tunnel. The creature took long flying jumps, getting closer and closer.

But there was no escape ahead of them. A few meters into the tunnel, five cars had overturned in the lane. They were on fire, the flames so high they reached the ceiling of the tunnel, forming an impassable barrier. From that glowing wall emerged a beast with a goat's head and a big human skull as a torso. Its beard and horns were made of tongues of fire. On its forehead, one could clearly see a five-pointed star, emitting red flashes.

A Luciferal.

As Egil hit the brakes, the lion closed on the sedan. Arian avoided teeth and claws with the elegance of a ballerina during a recital. This time, her bullets went through the lion's defenses, but their trajectory was interrupted by the quick movements of Augustine's crosier.

"Get back inside!" shouted Egil.

Before doing so, Arian fired one more time, grazing the Saint on his cheekbone.

"Hold on tight!" ordered the ex-military driver, accelerating at full speed.

"Are you crazy?" yelled Sabino. "We are going to crash against the Luciferal! We are all going to die!"

The skull on the torso of the horrible creature opened its mouth. Egil pushed a button on the side of the steering wheel, and suddenly the car accelerated.

"Have faith," said Arian to Sabino, grinning as she was pressed against the backrest by the high speed. "When you have faith, nothing is impossible!"

From the jaws of the skull came a wave of fire aiming at the sedan. Before it was too late, Egil swerved and climbed the left side of the tunnel vault, leaving the Luciferal behind. The white winged lion and Augustine were hit hard by the wave, while the sedan sped out of the tunnel.

"Minchia, this is driving!" Ciccio shouted. "We stuck it you-know-where to both the lion and the goat!"

"I think it's clear that the Luciferals are also looking for relics, if they're coming out of the woodwork," said Arian.

"As if we needed more to deal with," Ciccio grumbled, changing the magazines of his guns.

Still uneasy, Arian looked back. The tunnel was completely engulfed in flames. The goat-headed monster emerged, spread its wings, and flew toward them.

"Such a cutie!" commented Egil, accelerating once again. "It doesn't want us to leave… It likes us."

The speedometer needle marked over one hundred twenty-four miles per hour. Even so, the beast was getting closer and closer, spewing fire balls.

"All right, I am ready." Arian took out her guns, looking at Ciccio.

The car swerved to the side to avoid two burning balls, which exploded into the left lane.

"Let's go!" said Ciccio standing up on his seat. "Let's show them who is in charge!"

"No matter what happens, you and Sabino need to get to Cascia," Arian told Egil.

She read in the boy's eyes an ancestral fear of being alone, or worse, the dread that something terrible could happen to them. She deliberately looked away: he had to fend for himself against his fears.

Ciccio climbed on the roof, squatted, and then took a leap upward. His arms became covered in feathers and down, and his legs transformed into talons. Arian also jumped, and with an agile somersault landed on the enormous eagle's back.

The Luciferal flapped its wings and aimed at the eagle: it was so close that the heat it emanated was becoming unbearable. Arian soared upward, suspended in the air, as Ciccio dove toward the ground, avoiding a collision with the burning horns.

Arian unloaded her guns, riddling the monster's back with bullets, which bounced off like hailstones on the asphalt. In response, the skull on its chest spewed fire at the eagle; Ciccio spun to avoid the rainfall of flames, then soared beneath Arian. She landed on the back of the bird, which veered again to avoid another attack from the hellish creature. "Our old goat does not appreciate alchemical silver," she considered, "but I think I know what it does like."

The Luciferal stopped. The skull began to spew fire balls toward them.

"Let's get closer, Ciccio!"

As soon as they reached the right distance, she fired. The beast's forehead was pierced in two spots, and boiling lava leaked from the wounds. With a deep scream, the Luciferal rushed toward Arian.

The creature tried to bite, swallow, or simply burn her but it was all in vain. Arian anticipated all of its moves. Angry beyond belief, the monster focused its flames in the skull's mouth.

A third eye shimmered into existence on Arian's forehead. A far away voice made its way into her consciousness…

"Lucy?" she murmured, feeling enveloped in a warm maternal hug.

As the wind lashed her face, a whisper comforted her:

"I am here next to you.

All you have to do is look,

and with our eyes we will see the punishment of the wicked."

Arian leapt into the air, surrounded by light.

A hail of bullets rained on the creature, and the skull, reduced to a sieve, fell apart. Only the screaming head of the goat, in flames, was left. The woman knew her mission well. She closed her third eye and fired. The bullet reached the center of the lava pentacle in the goat's forehead, which exploded with incredible violence.

"Goodbye!" she shouted, making the sign of the cross and landing back on the eagle.

Black clouds of smoke rose skyward, and drops of lava plummeted down like meteors.

IX

Town of Sant'Anatolia (province of Perugia)

The blue sedan sped around the mountain bends. Sabino was experiencing an endless nausea, alternating gags and deep breaths while holding a paper bag.

"Slow down, Egil," he implored. "I think..."

The knight finally granted his request, which had been voiced several times, and downshifted.

"Thank you, bro!"

As soon as he said it, he threw up in the bag.

"Gross, picciò!" exclaimed Ciccio disgusted. The two Martyrs had caught up, slightly singed but no worse for the wear, after their battle with the Luciferal. They seemed unbothered by the snaking roads that sent Sabino's stomach roiling.

Looking up, Sabino groaned, "I asked you for a fucking pill against car sickness, but you—"

"What do you think we are? A drugstore?" said Arian, bursting into laughter.

"Can you at least tell me why we didn't take the highway? These turns are killing me!" continued Sabino. He was feeling weaker and weaker.

"There are no highways leading to Cascia," explained Egil.

"Understood, man! But we left the highway four hours ago. Four hours ago." He stabbed his knee with his finger to emphasize the repetition. "Four hours of fucking little roads full of fucking bends! Anyone would have thrown up! And we lost a bunch of time!"

"Listen to me, amico!" Egil ordered, his voice terse. "If the Chrismatics didn't know where we were heading and what car we were driving, now, after the chaos with the lion and the Luciferal, they certainly do. All eyes are on us. We couldn't risk finding a roadblock at the toll booth. That is why we left the highway. Understand?"

"I am sorry," Sabino groaned, his stomach upset with more than just the roads. "I fucked up." His heart was racing with guilt.

"Let's stop, please," suggested Arian, holding his forehead. "I think a break will be good for everyone."

"Damn it, Arian!" cursed Egil, taking yet another bend at full speed. "We cannot waste our time being his babysitter! Luciferals and Chrismatics are on our heels!"

"True, but if we keep this way, we are going into a ravine," Ciccio said dryly. "Amunìnne picciò, let's stop for a moment. I need a cigarette."

Egil rolled his eyes, giving up. With a sudden swerve, he parked the car.

"Congrats! We blew up the mission! Are you happy now?" He got out of the car to open Sabino's door. "What are you waiting for? We are leaving in two minutes!"

But Sabino could not answer. He was shaking, still holding the bag.

"Help him out," suggested Arian, opening her door. "He's about to throw up again."

Shaking his head, the knight took Sabino in his arms.

"How much do you weight? And you stink really badly, you know?" Egil groused as he carried Sabino away from the car toward a field of daisies.

"Look at him, Arian!" chuckled Ciccio, lighting a cigarette. "Isn't he a perfect daddy?"

"Shut up!" shouted Egil without turning around.

He laid his charge on the grass full of daisies. Sabino was already feeling better. The mountain air was good for him.

"Boy, it is easy to tell that you need discipline. Have you done your military service?"

"Well, no, not yet," Sabino said, though obviously he would—the law dictated it. "But I would like to."

A few bees buzzed around him.

"You would learn how to face difficulties and how to foresee dangers," Egil said, breathing out a puff of frustration. "Who knows, maybe you could learn to think before you speak."

"Leave him alone, picciò!" said Ciccio who had joined them. "He is saying all of this because he was a fanatic of a soldier, lo capisti?"

"How come you left the army?" asked Sabino.

Egil smiled. "A few years ago I was a pilot for NATO. I flew planes and helicopters, drove military vehicles, tanks…"

"So cool."

"Eventually I became the commander of a team of seven men. We were like brothers, and everything was going well, until…"

His face fell, and his voice dropped, grave.

"What happened?" Sabino pressed.

"Our platoon was in Lod, Israel. In the surrounding areas, there were a lot of groups of guerillas who liked to get into fights. One day, as we were patrolling, we located the hideout of a dangerous terrorist group. We should have called for reinforcements, but if we waited, they could have escaped and run away. We couldn't risk losing them…"

He stopped, lost in thoughts, quietly admiring the landscape. Sabino noticed that the cool breeze was making the daisies sway lightly.

"So?" Sabino prompted him, his nausea forgotten.

"We ventured into the cave where they were hiding. A long and winding tunnel, full of paintings on the walls. When I told Arian about it, she said it might have been an Early Christian catacomb, near a town once called Lydda."

"And then?"

"So much for hunters…We were the prey. There were about fifty of them, and we were soon surrounded. We tried with all our might to defend ourselves, but to no avail. One by one, all my comrades were badly wounded, and at the end I too…"

"No! Please don't tell me…"

"Yes, unfortunately." Egil's voice trembled slightly. "I wasn't able to get up or shoot. They immediately pounced on me and told me that, if I cooperated, my life would be spared. They were filming me, and they wanted me to ask their government to grant their requests. Then, I would have to deny my faith and my country. I can't describe the guilt I felt then toward my comrades, there, on the ground…It was then I understood what the right thing to do was."

Egil gave the middle finger with his right hand.

"Uagliò, man, you are a legend!" Sabino exclaimed.

"I don't think I have ever been so proud of my culture and my origins as I was at that moment. There was nothing that could have made me deny them. Since they saw I wasn't changing my mind, they threw me against the altar and hit me on the head four times. My eyesight blurred. I could only see red…a red and intense light. I know, it is hard to believe but, in that light I saw, or maybe I was dreaming about it, a huge dragon with an armored knight who was holding his hand out to me. Then nothing more until I woke up."

On the man's index finger, a ladybug landed. Shortly after, a new gust of wind blew it away.

"I was in a bed," he continued, "fully recovered. Next to me there was an old man. His name was Matusalem. He said he had dreamt of an angel telling him where to find me. And I realized I was wearing this relic around my neck."

"I am really sorry about your comrades," said Sabino. He was feeling stronger, as if that tale of heroism had given him a good dose of courage.

"The break is over!" They all turned to Arian who was rushing toward them. "I went patrolling, and a bit further ahead, just before entering Cascia, there is a roadblock. They are heavily armed. We might be able to get through, but we would be followed and we wouldn't be able to speak with the Abbess."

"Damn it!" Ciccio stomped back toward the sedan, letting out a string of curses. Sabino and Egil stood up and walked together to the car.

"It is likely there are other roadblocks, not just this one," Arian reflected. "There are going to be roadblocks on every road leading to town…How did they figure out we were coming here? Are there bugs? Are they following us? Or perhaps Bishop Boenzi said something…"

"Hey there, you! Do you need help?"

A chirpy voice came unexpectedly from above. Sabino looked up toward the peak of the mountain and saw a man with his grazing sheep.

"Oh my! The car has broken down, eh?" he continued, chuckling. "Let me come and give you a hand."

He began the descent, jumping from one rock to the next with incredible agility, as if he were one of his sheep.

"It's okay," replied Egil, uneasy. "The car is fine. Don't worry."

It was clear that the shepherd didn't hear him because he kept on coming toward them.

"What the minchia does he want?" growled Ciccio, nervously snapping his fingers. "We don't know him. I am going to teach him to mind his own business."

"No, just wait," said Arian. "Let's not draw attention, or those at the roadblock with alert everyone."

The stranger had reached the road and was now walking toward the group with a friendly smile. He wasn't tall, but his stern features would have kept more than one hothead away. His salt and pepper beard and his gnarled cane made him look like a man who had gone through a lot. He wore a gray cap and a black velvet jacket. The chain of a pocket watch decorated his vest.

"Hello! My name is Gianluca," he introduced himself. Pointing to each of the sheep, he continued: "This is Adelina, that is Beatrice, and then there is…"

"Minchia!" Ciccio was losing his patience. "Crazy! Crazy man!"

While Arian was trying to calm Ciccio down, Sabino stepped forward looking tough.

"DJ S.P. says hello to you and your friends."

"Wow! What a pleasure it is to know you, D.J.S.P.," replied Gianluca, saying each letter slowly. "And what are your friends' names?"

"Nice to meet you, Gianluca," said Arian quickly, squeezing the shepherd's hand. "My name is Lucia." Then, looking at the others, she continued, "This is Giorgio and Francesco."

"Good," said Gianluca. "So, what is wrong with your car?"

"The car is okay," repeated Egil. "We don't need help."

"That's a good one!" replied Gianluca looking at the torn roof. "So, would that be a new model of convertible car? What are you saying? It is obvious that you need a good mechanic, at least."

Ciccio was about to explode. "My friend, why don't you mind your f—"

"When we ran the numbers," said hastily Arian, "we realized it was going to be very expensive to take the car to the mechanic. So, we are waiting for our friends, who are very good at repairing cars. They will fix it for us, right boys?"

Egil nodded, staring the bizarre shepherd up and down. Ciccio, restrained by Arian, calmed enough down to keep his reactions under control.

"All right then!" said Gianluca, smiling. "You are all set! Just as well. I'll go back to my sheep."

He walked away, but when he reached the base of the rock ridge, he called out, "If you need any help, call me. I will be there in a heartbeat, my hand to God."

The cigarette butt fell from Ciccio's lips. The others looked at each other in amazement.

Sabino glanced at them in confusion. "Wait, what?"

"Hand to God," Arian explained. "Like Hand *of* God, our sect. It's a code."

"Signor Gianluca!" Egil called him back.

The shepherd meandered toward them again. "Very well, what do you need? Tell me."

"You see," started Arian, "we were sent by Digitus Secundus, and we need to see Abbess Cinzia of the convent of Saint Rita. Since you are from here, would you know when visiting hours end? The car breaking down will make us late…"

The shepherd removed his hat and slowly knelt.

"The door is always open for you, Martyrs. I feel so honored to have met you. I would like…"

"Please," Egil interrupted him, "we really need to see her."

"Amunìnne, picciò! Come on, up, up," urged Ciccio, helping Gianluca to get up.

The shepherd put his cap back on and mumbled, "I am sorry. You know, this is so emotional for me. Follow me."

They walked along a narrow path, barely visible, running along the rock wall.

"The convent should be behind us," observed Arian, concerned. "Where are we going?"

"Didn't you see?" explained Gianluca, gesturing. "The town is heavily guarded. We wouldn't be able to set foot there without the Chrismatics being immediately after us."

"And so, where are we going?"

"Here," he announced, moving aside the thorny branches of a large blackberry bush. In front of him stood the entrance to a hidden tunnel.

"From here you get to the convent," he added. "This is an old escape route, known only to us of the brotherhood."

"Fantastic!" Sabino was hyper. "Great, give me a high five!" he said, raising his palm in front of the shepherd.

Gianluca ignored the gesture and, turning on a flashlight, entered the secret passage. The Martyrs followed him without paying too much attention to the fourth member of the group.

"Hey! Wait for me!" said Sabino, entering last.

The narrow tunnel went deeper and deeper into the mountain. The dancing light of their flashlights revealed numerous rivulets of water on the walls. Amid the silence, Sabino noticed that Egil was keeping an eye on Ciccio. Perhaps he did not want another accident like the one in Padua.

After about half an hour of stumbling in the dark, the shepherd stopped and pointed his light upward. The cold beam showed a hollow in the low ceiling where one could clearly see a marble slab.

"You get inside the convent from there," Gianluca explained. "We are exactly under the Abbess's meditation cell."

"Minchia," Ciccio's voice was hoarse and panting. "Let's get out of here. I can't..."

"Of course!" Gianluca said. "The agreed signal is to knock three times on the slab."

"I'll do it," said Arian, climbing on Egil's shoulders.

Once she followed the instructions, the slab shifted, dropping some dust and rubble. When it was lifted, a warm light flooded the gloomy tunnel.

Gianluca's eyes shone with emotion. "Go! Oh, this is the happiest day of my whole life!"

The Martyrs climbed through the trapdoor. The shepherd took Sabino in his arms and lifted him so that his friends, from above, could grab him.

"What about you? Aren't you coming?" asked Sabino.

"My mission ends here. I am not allowed to enter a convent for women. Pray for us."

Sabino thanked him as the others pulled him up.

X

Cascia (province of Perugia). Convent of Saint Rita

In a small, bare room, a slender figure welcomed the four Martyrs as they emerged from the tunnel.

"Welcome, pilgrims. I am Mother Cinzia, abbess of this convent."

She wore monastic robes and had a huge wooden cross around her neck. Sabino noticed that the necklace had gold foils.

"Tell me, please, who are you and where do you come from?" asked the abbess watching them carefully.

"Digitus Secundus sends us," replied Arian, showing her the silver ring baring the carving with the eye within the triangle. The others did the same with their own relics.

"For Baphomet's beard! It is really you!" proclaimed Mother Cinzia, examining them. And then to Sabino: "You are Alessandro's nephew, aren't you?"

The boy lit up. "Yes, ma'am. Do you have any news about him? How is he doing?"

"Unfortunately, I only know what they say on TV. He is in critical condition."

Sabino looked down and instinctively thought that perhaps he should leave the convent and his fellow travelers to join his uncle Alex. Then, he remembered that his current situation had changed quite a bit. He was a Martyr and even, to some, the Anti-Christ. He had lost his freedom, maybe forever. He began to miss his previous life, when he was anonymous, when his days were just like those of many other teenagers.

"I know your uncle well," said the abbess. "He is a strong man; he will make it. Please, close the access to the tunnel and follow me. Time is running out."

Ciccio moved the marble slab back into its original position, quietly, closing the secret passage.

"Good. I'll take you to my private chamber. Do not speak to anyone, and keep quiet," she ordered.

From the pocket of her robes, she took out a large key and opened the door, which led to a corridor barely lit by candle. Echoes of liturgical singing could be heard all around, heightening the feeling of sacredness inspired by the place itself. They walked without ever turning around, along rows of doors that all looked alike. Eventually, they stopped in front of a double door. The abbess walked in first, telling them to take their seat and locking them all inside.

The room was sizeable; the walls with shelves overflowing with books. A large crucifix hung on the wall opposite the entrance, above a massive walnut desk. The floor was covered by a blood red carpet, decorated with dark figures that reminded Sabino of those boring scenes painted on ancient Roman vases. Or were they Greek?

Abbess Cinzia took a seat behind her desk and said, "My courageous Martyrs, I was able to prevent the Chrismatics from entering the convent, but they relentlessly patrol the outside. They certainly have suspicions."

"It is really strange," said Arian. "How could they have known we were coming here? The only explanation I can think of is that Bishop Boenzi…"

"He is dead," announced Abbess Cinzia, closing her eyes as if wanting to pray.

"Bastards!" exclaimed Ciccio in a moment of rage. "Did they torture him?"

"I don't think so… The news reported something about poisoning, and said the culprit for the damages at the cathedral was a Luciferal with monkish features."

Sabino looked at Ciccio, who was about to light a cigarette. How was he able to let everything wash over him time after time? Even though Sabino barely knew the bishop, he was very sorry for his death. Would the four of them live up to Boenzi's expectations? What if the bishop had sacrificed himself in vain?

"We need to be strong," said Egil. "If we don't succeed, his death was for nothing."

The abbess rushed to open a few drawers, taking out a couple of big boxes.

"There are some vials here," she explained, opening the one on the left. "They were part of the convent's treasures, but I believe you will make better use of them. This one has a precious and rare substance: manna, very nutritious, a real cure-all for wounds. It is not easy to come by. This one is holy water. Sometimes it is the only remedy against the Luciferals."

"So cool! And in the other box?" asked Sabino very enthusiastically.

"Bullets made using alchemy. The Sons of Joseph of Arimathea worked a lot to make them."

"This is exactly what we need!" exclaimed Arian. "I was almost out of magazines."

Excited, she rushed to rummage through the box reviewing its contents: "Plumbeum… Stannum… Ferrum… Cuprum… Hydroargentum… Argentum…"

"You should be able to wound any opponent with these," Abbess Cinzia said. "We tried every way possible to forge Aurum, the powerful alchemical gold, but we failed."

"Alche… gold… what?" Sabino was bewildered.

"Alchemical gold," explained Arian, gathering her magazines. "It means that the bullets are crafted by hand, following very ancient metalworking treaties, so that the process purifies the element contained in them."

"Element?" Sabino repeated. "Are you saying that an alchemical bullet has only one element—lead?"

"Yes," Abbess Cinzia said, picking up where Arian had left off. "Alchemy aims to purify the six elements in the metals influenced by the six planets. *Plumbeum,* Saturn's metal, is the alchemical version of the common lead, and has within it the alchemical energy of the element of darkness. *Ferrum,* Mars's metal, is linked to the element earth and so on and so forth. The elements create the metals, not the other way around."

"This is mind-blowing!"

"These notions are actually very helpful," Arian went on. "Each element is in opposition to another. Think about the Chrismatics: they are essentially made of the element of light. With one single

Plumbeum bullet, which is pure darkness… Bang! Gone. If instead you try to shoot a normal bullet…"

"Class dismissed, picciò!" Ciccio cut the lesson short. "Abbess Cinzia, let's discuss an important point: where is the Grail?"

"I don't know," she replied, rummaging through another drawer.

Ciccio began to cough, puffing clouds of smoke.

"Abbess Cinzia," Egil interjected, resting his hands on the desk, "you must know something! Bishop Boenzi told us you would show us the place—"

"Excuse me," the abbess interrupted him, "I need a hand."

Sabino went behind the desk and saw she was struggling with the drawers: she had completely taken one out and was trying to take a thick, ancient-looking tome out of some sort of double-bottom. He helped her remove the volume and place it on the table with a thud.

"The answer to your question is in here," she announced solemnly.

Arian walked over to examine the volume. It had a hard wooden cover and a large number of parchment sheets corroded by time. On the cover, the dust obscured an inscription in Greek: APOSTOLWN PRAXEIS.

"The Acts of the Apostles! What do they have to do with this?" she asked, incredulous.

"These are the Acts of the Apostles of Joseph of Arimathea, the custodians of the Grail," explained the abbess.

"Ok, but where is the Grail?" prompted Ciccio. "Minchia, we don't have the time to read that whole thing!"

"Actually," continued Abbess Cinzia, "this codex contains only part of the Acts of the Apostles of Joseph, the one that explains where the Holy Grail is. The second part, where it tells you how to get it once you get to the exact location, is kept by Bishop Centritto, in Naples."

Arian was trying hard to open the volume but to no avail. It seemed sealed.

"Save your energy. No one can read that text. Only those who have entered in communion with the Shroud can open the holy seal imposed by Joseph's Apostles."

The three Martyrs turned to Sabino.

"Me?!"

"If the Almighty so willed, so be it!" uttered the abbess. "Come on!"

The boy fearfully approached the volume. He was about to extend his hands, but he immediately pulled back. After a few seconds of hesitation, he rubbed them on his pants. Finally, he placed his shaking hands on the cover. He tried to open it, but it felt glued on. He tried to force it, prying open the sheets. Nothing worked. The tome looked like a single indivisible slab of marble.

"I can't do it," he concluded, dejected, leaving the big volume on the table.

"Yes, you can," replied Arian, placing a hand on his arm. "You just have to want it."

Sabino looked at the book as if to study its weak points.

"Amunìnne picciò!" Ciccio urged. "Show that book who you are! Minchia, come on, show your faith!"

Sabino approached it again and stretched out his left hand toward the cover. *I can do it… I must do it… I want to do it,* he thought.

He closed his eyes.

I will do it!

The white bandana around his arm sparkled with the brightest of light. As if by magic, the heavy wooden cover moved, followed by dozens of sheets. Inside the volume, a secret compartment revealed an ancient papyrus.

"I did it!" shouted Sabino jumping up and down. "I did it! DJ S.P. rocks! Give me five, my friends!"

"You rock, Sabino!" Egil hugged him tightly.

Abbess Cinzia approached him and knelt before him, moved.

"The power of the Almighty has manifested itself here, in front of us! I thank you, Lord, for allowing me to witness such a miracle. At last, the secret kept for centuries by our predecessors is in the hands of the one who can reach the Apotheosis."

"What?" asked the boy, worried, freeing himself from his friend's hug.

"The Apotheosis is your objective, Martyrs," replied the abbess. "Thanks to the power of the Grail, you will revive Christ and avert the madness of Armageddon that Peter II is planning."

"Eureka!" Arian's voice sounded crystal clear when she spoke. She had been absorbed reading the papyrus now unrolled on the desk. "Listen to this…"

All of them, full of curiosity, walked over to her.

Sabino noticed that the incomprehensible writing on the papyrus was glowing with the same white light enveloping his bandana. "'I, Paolo Amico, servant of God, of Christ and Apostle of Joseph of Arimathea—'"

"Wonderful!" Abbess Cinzia said, happy. "Tradition records him as one of the most influential figures among Joseph's disciples."

Arian continued: "'—and custodian of the Holy Grail, write these words inspired by the vision of the Almighty. On this day, 31 October 1239 in the Year of Our Lord, God has manifested Himself to me…' Hey, what?"

Under the stunned eyes of all present, the light of the writing began to fade until it vanished completely.

"The Shroud!" exclaimed the abbess. "The Shroud has stopped shining!"

Sabino looked at his arm. It did.

"It could make sense," confirmed Arian. "The light of the Shroud allows us to read the papyrus. No light, no writing."

"Try again," the abbess begged him.

"I already did it once. Now it should be easy-peasy," the boy lied to himself. The stares of the others made him feel under pressure.

"Don't worry, DJ S.P. takes care of it!"

Faking confidence, he extended his arm.

Nothing. The papyrus stayed white.

I can do it… I must do it… I want to do it.

"They are reappearing!" exulted the abbess. "The writing is reappearing! Praise the Lord!"

In a cold sweat, the boy tried not to get distracted by the celebrations. He had to think about the paper. He had to make the writing appear again, just like in school…

"Keep it up…" Arian encouraged him.

Keep it up, Pignataro, and you will repeat the year!

Suddenly, the voice of his Italian literature teacher boomed in his head. He saw again, her disappointed expression on her wrinkled face and the red mark on his paper: 20%

Do you know what you really deserve? Zero! Nothing more.

"Zero!" he also shouted.

He slumped to the ground with his eyes wide open.

"…the power of the Shroud is too strong for him."

Confused voices crowded Sabino's ringing ears while the world around him slowly resumed its shape.

"Let's give him time. He hasn't received proper training yet."

Arian's voice snapped him out of his numbness. He realized he was on his back on the floor.

"The papyrus! Are we able to read it?" he asked, sitting up.

"Nope," replied Egil.

"So, what should we do now?" continued Sabino. His head was spinning.

Abbess Cinzia looked him straight in the eye. "The papyrus isn't enough, young Martyr, nor is it enough to know where the Grail is. It is necessary to know how to recover it. And only Bishop Centritto in Naples can help you."

Sabino nodded. He was still terribly confused. "Abbess Cinzia, before I leave, I need to know something… How can we revive Christ? And if we are not able to? And why is it that the Saints call me Anti-Christ? What am I really? If I am not the Anti-Christ, why are they after us?"

"You must have faith," replied the woman, seraphic.

"Calm down, Sabino. Come on," added Arian, reassuringly.

Sabino felt he was about to explode. "I can't! You need to explain everything to me first! What is Good? And Evil? I can't understand all of this. I…"

"Repent all of you!"

The eyes of the crucifix on the wall were wide open and glowing with light.

"Repent, while there is still time!" added the statue, moving as if wanting to come down.

Suddenly, two gunshots pierced Christ: one in the center of his forehead and the other one in his heart. His eyes went dead, and his head fell limply to one side.

Arian had shot him.

"They have found us!" The abbess was terrified. "Run, quickly!"

Sabino rushed to the door. As soon as he touched the handle, though, it transformed into a tangle of thorny branches.

“Move!” shouted Arian as she discharged her magazines against the thorns, where some rose buds were opening. The tangle, however, was unaffected by the bullets, instead growing to cover the walls, choking the room. An intense sweet scent spread to every corner.

“Do not breathe!” ordered Egil, bringing a handkerchief to his nose. “Abbess Cinzia, is there another way out?”

When he turned toward the abbess, he found her slumped on the floor, unconscious, and maybe dead.

In the meantime, Ciccio had been replaced with a bloodshot-eyed brown bear, pouncing on the brambles that were blocking the door. His mighty paws uprooted several branches, but he couldn’t create an opening. The beast began to bleed, and his blows became weaker and weaker.

“Come back!” shouted Arian, covering her face as best as she could with a handkerchief.

It was too late. After one last pawing, the animal fell to the floor, prone, and was immediately covered in flowering brambles.

The room had turned into a kind of hollow bush, dotted with very fragrant red roses.

Sabino followed the example of the others and covered his face, but the sweet aroma crept into his nostrils, making him nauseous. His head was heavy; every noise sounded far and muffled, and a dull, regular sound, like a heartbeat, became increasingly clear.

He found himself lying on the floor, his eyes lost in the void as rose petals fell from above. *Tum-tum, tum-tum, tum-tum.*

He closed his eyes, captivated by the rhythm of the beat.

Tum-tum, tum-tum, tum-tum.

The sound was warm, like the hug from a loved one.

Tum-tum, tum-tum, tum-tum.

"Sabino?" A soft voice reached his ears. "Wake up…"

He opened his eyes and saw a feminine face, with delicate features. She smiled sweetly.

"Heaven be praised! How wonderful to be able to hold you again, my darling," said the woman, hugging him close.

Those features looked familiar. They reminded him of his mother, whom he had admired many times in photos.

"Mom! Is it really you?"

"Yes, we are finally together. Are you happy?"

A tear rolled down Sabino's cheek as he embraced her with all his strength. Rose petals kept raining down from the sky.

"Stand up, let me look at you!" she urged him, helping him up. "My God! You have grown so much!"

Sabino stared at her blue eyes, barely open in the emotional moment, and noticed that she was wearing a dark dress with a black veil over her head that made her look like a nun. As Uncle Alex had told him, she had dressed like that since the day her husband died. At the center of her bandaged forehead, he noticed a red spot.

"Mom, what happened to you? Did you bang your head?"

"No, not at all," replied the woman smiling. "The Almighty allowed me to participate in His suffering this way."

It was strange that his uncle had never mentioned that detail to him before.

"My sufferings have been repaid. I thought I would never see you again, and instead here you are!"

"I am very happy. But where have you been, Mom? Because…"

Suddenly, Sabino almost stumbled. He looked down and saw that, by his feet, there was a bear's head poking out from the sea of red petals that covered the floor. Fighting a feeling of surprise mixed with fear, he bent down to have a better look. It seemed familiar…

"Come on, come with me," said his mother, taking his hand. "I'll make you something nice to eat. You must be hungry, I bet."

The two walked down a bright and long path. On the left, Sabino noticed a crucifix on which a salt and pepper man was nailed. His military clothes had bloodstains, and he was almost entirely covered by roses and thorns. The horror that Sabino felt was overcome by a doubt: where had he seen that man before?

"Who is he?" he asked, stopping.

"It doesn't matter. Let's go."

Up ahead, on the right side, a half-naked woman was also crucified. Her red braids were full of roses and thorns. Her python-themed clothes were torn where the spines had pierced her flesh. Her dark sunglasses were covered in blood.

The sweet scent of flowers was getting more pungent. Sabino felt that his head was about to burst.

"Arian!" he shouted, letting go of his mother's hand and running toward the crucifix.

"My son, come back here!" his mother shouted. "We need to go home."

"Help me, Mom! I recognize them! These are my friends! I must save them!"

He tried in vain to pull off some rose branches, hurting his hands.

"Forget them! They aren't your friends at all. They were only using you to accomplish their evil purposes."

Sabino was shocked. Myriad conflicting thoughts flooded his mind.

"But… Uncle," he stuttered. "He said…"

"Even Bishop Bafunno was corrupted by the flattery of the enemy," lamented the woman. "So far you have acted against the work of God, the Invincible. You have been instigated by these heretical sinners."

"No, Mom! I have to save them, please!"

"The Almighty's justice is unavoidable. Have faith! The destiny that awaits them is far better than the one Bishop Bafunno faced."

Sabino froze. "Something happened to Uncle Alex?"

"He has been excommunicated. Hell's flames and torments await him."

"Who cares about the excommunication!" Sabino shouted. "How is he? Is he better?"

"I don't care about his health," his mother sniffed. "Come on, come with me!"

The boy was distraught. Unclear images swirled in his head. Arian's smile. Egil's hug. Ciccio saving him and Uncle Alex from the fire. His mom, found again after so long, holding out her hand to him. And his uncle's last words: "The Martyrs."

"No," he replied, determined, as his left arm glowed white. "DJ S.P. is not going to betray his friends."

He tightened his grip around a branch wrapping Arian's mangled body and closed his eyes as thorns made their way under his skin, tearing it.

"My darling, please," his mother begged. "Yours is a futile effort."

Sabino was no longer listening to the woman veiled in black. A wave of light ran through the brambles, starting at his bleeding hands.

When he opened his eyes, he was in the abbess's room and a sparkling dust was falling from the ceiling. On the carpet, lying down, there were Arian, Egil, a brown bear, and Abbess Cinzia. Gone were the roses and the thorns.

A brutal slap sent him flying across the room into a wall; books teetered from the shelves with an annoying thud.

"You brat!" the woman told him. "You were a very bad boy!"

She grabbed him by his hair and began to slap and punch him. Sabino wasn't able to react, he felt guilty for having made his mother angry.

"Are you done now, son?"

Without giving him the chance to answer, she dragged him across the floor to the stunned bodies of the others.

"Look what you are making me do," she said. "These wretches could have died peacefully and gone to Heaven, but you wanted to deprive them of such a privilege... Why did you believe their lies instead of having faith in the Almighty?"

In her palm appeared a withered rose.

"Do you know what this is? The Dry Rose. It quickly drains the life of those it touches, marring them with excruciating pain. This is the punishment your false friends are about to receive."

"N...no," mumbled Sabino, exhausted.

"It is your fault! Only your fault. I will start with this little bitch..."

The woman threw the dried flower, which leapt very quickly toward Arian. But Sabino's outstretched hand deflected its trajectory, drawing it close to him. With a hissing sound, the sharp stem stabbed Sabino in his palm. He cried in pain as the bandana on his arm lit up. With a swift movement, the Dry Rose extracted itself from Sabino's palm and went to pierce his opponent's chest.

"You, degenerate son," she cursed in an altered voice. "How dare you commit such a folly? You will not get off easily this time."

She placed her hand on the flower in order to remove it, but the stem wouldn't budge; it had begun turning green.

"Mercy!" she cried.

Slowly, her appearance changed. Her eyes became watery, and deep wrinkles branched across her face.

"You are just like one of my children, not only in appearance but also in spirit," she whispered, in a heartbreaking wail, as her teeth fell out. "I hoped I could save you by keeping you with me, but your heart is hopelessly corrupt by the Devil's flattery."

Sabino couldn't fathom her metamorphosis and felt a mixture of disappointment and relief: that was not his mom, as he had hoped. It was better this way.

"Listen, O Lord, the prayer of your humble servant, Rita, patroness of this convent!" cried the Saint as the Dry Rose in her chest turned fully green and lush. "I beg you: destroy me and this unclean race!"

The woman's head exploded with an unprecedented violence.

The explosion quickly spread to all the rooms of the convent. Everything went up in flames. Like a huge house of cards, the old building collapsed with a terrible roar.

XI

CASCIA • 6:21 PM

The light was so warm it took his breath away.

"Mom, no… I don't want to hurt you… Don't go after them…"

A flock of doves took flight, disappearing into the light.

Then, darkness.

Slowly, Sabino opened his eyes to confused and blurred images.

"…ke …up …bi …no."

Distant sounds of a faded memory.

"Wake up, Sabino!"

Instinctively, Sabino blocked the merciless hand that was about to slap him again.

"Shit, but will you st—"

He opened his eyes wide in amazement and his sentence died in his throat.

"I knew you would come around!" Arian drew him closer to her, holding to him very tightly. Sabino, still groggy, thought he was dreaming. He could feel the warmth of her body and the softness of her features.

Ciccio chuckled. "Picciò, don't get too excited, okay?"

"This is his magic moment, don't ruin it for him," said Egil towering over them.

"Praised be Jesus Christ!" concluded Abbess Cinzia.

Sabino looked around. He was in a damp rock tunnel lit by light red hue, the last rays of the setting sun.

"Where are we?"

"Further on, the underground passage comes out to the south of the village," replied the abbess, pointing to a big opening from which light was coming in.

Ciccio put out his cigarette with the heel of his shoe. "I'm going to look for a vehicle. Be ready, there is no time to lose."

With those words, he exited the tunnel. Egil walked over to Sabino placing a hand on his shoulder.

"I am ready!" Sabino assured him. "A bit achy, but I am ready!"

"Take it easy. I just wanted to thank you."

Sabino stilled under the weight of Egil's hand. "Me? Why?"

"You stood firm in your faith," Egil told him. "And not only did you stand up to Saint Rita, but you also sacrificed yourself for our safety."

Sabino's mind was suddenly flooded with terrible and painful memories. The Dry Rose… Helpless Arian… His mother's curse…

"In the darkness of pain," said Arian squeezing his hand, "I saw a very white light, and I felt that the Spirit of your relic was protecting me. Thank you, Sabino."

The boy stared at the Shroud, tied around his arm like a bandana. Arian's words reached him like far echoes.

"Thanks to your faith, we escaped the explosion. Alessandro would be proud of you!" added Abbess Cinzia.

He came to his senses. He couldn't bear not to have news of his uncle's health. But he couldn't lose hope.

If he did, he would be finished, once and for all.

Darkness fell with no sign of Ciccio. A dense vegetation hid the entrance to the tunnel, located on a steep slope a few feet above the road.

"It looks like there are no Christmatics around," said Arian. Even though it was dark, she wore her very dark sunglasses.

"Be careful not to slip!" Egil warned them.

A shy moon was peeking through the clouds as the Martyrs and the abbess walked cautiously through the vegetation. When they came close to the road, they squatted behind some bushes. They waited silently until they heard the rumble of a car approaching. They saw the headlights first, then the imposing outline of a big SUV speeding on the dangerous bends.

"What a showoff," commented Sabino. It was Ciccio for sure.

The massive car came to an abrupt halt and from the rolled-down window appeared a hand holding a cigarette.

"I knew it!"

"Captain Corleone invites you to come onboard his new ship," Ciccio announced. "Amunìnne, picciò, let's go."

Sabino, Egil and Arian hopped in.

"Come with us to Naples, Abbess!" suggested Egil.

"You go, valiant heroes of the faith. I will stay here to make sure that the Sons of Joseph are okay. I can't abandon them. Bishop Centritto will see you without any problems. You just need to say that it was Annularia who sent you. Go now and may God protect you!"

Ciccio stepped on the accelerator and the imposing SUV took off.

Sabino was already feeling nauseous. "Fuck, will you slow down? If you don't, I will throw up on the seat…"

"Okay, okay … But you can do whatever you want. This car is not mine anyway…"

"I only hope the owner realizes it is missing as late as possible. I don't want the police after us," said Arian.

Ciccio engaged a turn. "Don't worry, Arian, the convent collapsing has sent the whole village in a frenzy. The roadblocks have been dismantled. I really don't think they are going to care about a stolen car! Anyway, I heard that so far they have only recovered unidentifiable corpses. I think they are going to give us up for dead…"

"Very good!" Egil said with a firm nod.

Sabino signed with relief. *When a wanted person dies, no one hunts them any longer,* he thought.

He sank into the seat and half-closed his eyes, exhausted. For the first time since being with his friends, he felt he could finally relax. And, perhaps, even feel proud of himself.

"...next time we aren't going to be this lucky."

Sabino opened his eyes. The tone of the conversation did not foretell anything good.

"I concur," replied Arian from next to him, "but Sabino can't do much more than this."

"Are you talking about me?" he interjected, leaning forward between the two front seats.

He stared at them one by one. Arian, as always, was inscrutable behind her sunglasses. Ciccio smiled as if nothing was wrong. The only one who seemed worried was Egil.

"Yes, Sabino," he said, "we were talking also about you. As you may have seen, the power of the Saints is really extraordinary. We Martyrs do our best, but this last time we were seriously in danger of not making it..."

"You have already thanked me enough. DJ S.P. did great on all fronts, don't you think?" gloated Sabino.

"This is exactly it. You defended us from Saint Rita with great courage, but unfortunately it wasn't you who saved us from the convent's collapse," explained Arian.

"What do you mean? The—the light—it wasn't me?"

He couldn't believe it.

"A typical case of override…" Egil sighed.

"Overwhat?"

"Override is a term indicating a situation of imposition—*praevaricatio*. Simply put, your relic took over and decided for you. The Shroud used you as a means to accomplish *its* will," explained Arian.

Sabino looked in disbelief at the bandana around his arm. Up until then he never thought that object could think or even act on its own. Suddenly, he felt his stomach tighten by the claws of fear. He began to convulsively unravel the cloth from his wrist.

"I don't want it! This cloth thinks! And controls me! I do not want it."

"Don't waste your energy, picciò!" Ciccio chuckled, still driving around the bends. "Once a relic chooses us, we become one with it."

The truth hit him, and Sabino realized that his efforts were worthless. If he tried to untie the knots on one side, the bandana would immediately re-tie itself on the other. He began to sob.

"Come on, come here." Arian invited him into her arms.

Sabino didn't wait to be asked twice. He rushed to her, soaking her clothes with his warm tears. Slowly the steady beat of Arian's heart calmed him down. He remembered faded smells and feelings of a safe place.

Who knew? Maybe it felt like his real mother's hug.

Stroking his hair, Arian continued: "If the Shroud has chosen you, it means it likes you. Think of it as a sort of friend. A new friend with whom you need to learn to get along."

Sabino signed. Truth be told, the Shroud had never hurt him. And the idea of always having a friend on his forearm, after all… Yes, it was not so bad.

Gently, he pulled away from Arian's chest.

"I am sorry…" he whispered, his head lowered.

"Look at me," Arian told him.

Sabino looked up, almost hoping to be met with his mother's eyes, only to find his frowning reflection in Arian's glasses. "None of us accepted the relic easily," she said. "We trained hard to learn how to use their power effectively. I assure you it wasn't easy for any of us."

"That's it!" exclaimed Egil. He found his smile again. "This is what we need: a nice round of training! So Sabino will finally be able to master the Shroud's powers."

Arian nodded in agreement.

"Have you gone crazy?" objected Ciccio, making the car swing. "You really think that now is the time to turn around, go back to Bari, and let Bishop Grassano train him as he did with us? There is no way!"

"You're right." Egil exchanged a look of understanding with Arian. "We're going to train him," he finished.

"Who? You two?" Ciccio scoffed. "Don't make me laugh!"

"We'll make the best of the situation," replied Arian. "And

besides, for your information, I also hold a certificate for high school teaching."

"Combining your theoretical training with my years in the military, we will turn this recruit into the perfect Martyr in no time. What do you think, Sabino?" asked Egil.

Sabino was stupefied. On the one hand, the idea of mastering the Shroud was really appealing; on the other, he feared the training was going to be worse than school. He did not know how to answer, and he cast an unsure glance at Ciccio, who was chuckling in the rearview mirror.

"It doesn't matter what you are going to say, picciò… You are screwed now!"

XII

Twenty-four… twenty-five…"

Puffing, Sabino lifted himself up from the sandy ground with shaking arms. His face was purple with exertion. He gasped repeatedly.

"Come on!" Egil pushed him. "I didn't tell you to stop!"

"Let's not overdo it. This is his first day of training!" said Arian, worried.

"We don't have time!" replied Egil, walking with slow, cadenced steps around their trainee, leaving footprints in the beach. "We are presumed dead, this is true, but the patriarch must have realized we were looking for the Grail. We cannot let him get to it before us or allow him to find out who the other members of the Hand of God are…"

"Coming through…" Ciccio dragged a small boat across the sand.

"So, you're really going to fish?" asked Arian, mockingly.

"No, but I'm certainly not going to pester Sabino like you two are doing. I would have liked to buy the fishing gear, but everything around here is closed. Rather than calling this place 'Long Lake,' it should be called 'Dead Lake' instead."

"We chose a protected area precisely because no one will come here to ask questions. Now scram!" repeated Egil for the umpteenth time.

"Yes, sir!" shouted Ciccio, cigarette between his lips. He pushed the boat into the water and climbed in. Shortly after, he began to hum.

"Thirty!" shouted Sabino, drenched in sweat. His chest felt heavy and his arms so sore, but he was painting happily.

"This ends your physical training. He is all yours, Arian."

"I bet you are thirsty," said the woman to Sabino, handing him a water bottle.

He drank greedily. Then he rubbed his arm over his face to dry it. It was a gesture that made him feel rough and manly.

"Well, signore," Arian mocked him, "take off your shoes and follow me."

"Take off my shoes? Why?"

Arian smiled. "You are about to walk on water."

The sun's reflection on the lake was rippled by the water. A light breeze swayed the reeds on the shore. The silence was broken only by the croaking of dozens of tree frogs. Ciccio, in the middle of the lake, lay down, placidly sunbathing, in his small boat.

"The key to success is faith—that is, firmly believing that you can do something," said Arian, once again.

Sabino was terrified of drowning, as he'd never learned to swim. He sighed heavily. The boat, his established finishing line, looked so very far away. He rolled his jeans up to his knees and looked at the Shroud in his arm.

Arian read his mind. "Do not be afraid: it is your friend. You just need to find a way to get along."

Sabino timidly took a step with his left foot. Under the impassive eyes of his two instructors, his toes twitched as soon as they touched the water.

"But it is cold!" he complained, between sadness and disappointment.

He was met with an immediate glare by Egil. He sank his whole foot into the icy water.

"Come on, Shroud, help me out!"

His right foot joined the left underwater on a smooth stone covered in seaweed.

"Think you are light!" advised Arian from the shore, which now seemed so far away.

With his eyes closed, he lifted his left foot again. His heart raced. He was already thinking horrible scenarios, like sinking into watery depths, when his right foot slipped on the slimy stone. Screaming at the top of his lungs and squirming like a madman, he managed to hold himself up, splashing water all around. Dozens of frightened herons took flight among the reeds.

In no time, he rushed to the shore, gasping in fright.

"Calm down, calm down," Arian soothed him. "Your fears overtook you. You were afraid of something that did not happen, and because of this, you gave up on making something great happen."

Sabino could only agree with her. With his head down, he saw a white butterfly land on the woman's finger.

"If you really believe it, you can really do it. This young butterfly was a caterpillar for most of her life. What do you think she thought the first time her wings came out?"

Staring at the graceful extremities of the insect, Sabino replied, "Was she afraid? Did she feel she was unable to fly?"

Arian smiled. "Quite the opposite. She was totally unfazed. She had wings and flew away."

While he thought about those words, the butterfly took flight. Yes, he should live like she did: Light, carefree, and most of all free of fear. The insect skimmed the rippling water, then hovered in the air among the flowers' petals, before finally flying toward the reedbed.

It was then that the boy noticed the frog crouching on a surfacing rock.

He felt dead inside at the thought of that beautiful creature being sucked in the slimy jaws of that awful being.

"No!" he shouted reaching out his hand toward the reedbed.

In less than an instant, the long sticky tongue of the frog slammed against the back of his hand. The frog, disappointed, jumped into the lake croaking. Sabino looked around agitated. Where was his beloved butterfly? He heard a fluttering, and his shoulders loosened. The butterfly was there, safe and sound, wavering among the reeds.

"Excellent!" shouted Arian.

Sabino came to. How did he manage to get so distracted?

"Oh, I am sorry... I just took a little break..."

Egil shook his head, laughing. "My oh my! Didn't you realize you were walking on the water?"

Sabino winced. Stiff like a statue, he slowly lowered his eyes.

It was true. His feet were stable on the water's surface!

"Do not lose your concentration!" Arian shouted.

Sabino looked up again, resting his eyes on the Shroud. It was there on his wrist, glowing a faint whitish light.

"Remember that you and I are friends," he told it. "Don't abandon me now!"

He took a step. He could feel the water's surface under the soles of his feet like a thick layer of ice. Solid but slippery.

"Amunìnne, picciò—come on, boy! Do not waste your time chit-chatting! Get here before its effect wears off!" Ciccio called from the boat. He was sitting now, eagerly watching Sabino's progress.

Feeling better thanks to the support of his friends, Sabino ran, fast and without hesitation, creating waves just like a speedboat. When he passed the boat, he turned around, running back toward the shore.

"Look at me! The Shroud and I are one! We do incredible things!"

Egil and Arian gave each other a high five. Their smiles, however, died out when Sabino, curving abruptly in front of the shore, engulfed them in water and seaweed.

Ciccio guffawed. "You are my hero, picciò! Now come here until those two are no longer mad at you."

Sabino listened to Ciccio's advise. He accelerated to full throttle, only to brake suddenly in front of the boat, soaking Ciccio from head to toe. The huge man, drenched, cast him a very eloquent look.

"I am sorry," Sabino laughed, not sounding sorry at all. "I need to practice more."

Ciccio smiled a bigger smile than usual. Suddenly, his expression turned into pure horror. He pointed at something between Sabino's legs. The boy looked down and a powerful slap hit him on the head.

Under his feet, the thin layer that kept him on the surface broke, and Sabino fell into the water.

"Help!" he shouted, moving frantically. "I can't swim!"

Leaning forward, Ciccio retrieved him effortlessly. "You showed a weak spot to your enemy and lost your concentration. Not good, not good at all!"

Sabino coughed, spitting out water.

"Amunìnne, picciò! That's enough training for today. You did pretty well, but you made a moronic mistake at the end: the oldest trick in the world."

"But you…you said you didn't want to be a trainer."

The Sicilian half-smiled. "Remember these words of mine: training, like life, is a constant battle. And in war, you can only trust your relic."

XIII

About time! The water is boiling! Did you find the eggplants?"

Ciccio, from the middle of the kitchen, gestured in their direction with a big knife.

"Yes, chef!" Egil mocked him, placing two grocery bags on the kitchen table. "We had to go to six different stores as far away as Belmonte Castello to find all the ingredients. Couldn't you make a simpler dish?"

"Slow down, signore!" Ciccio replied. "You chose this little hamlet in the middle of the Ciociaria area. And it was you all who asked me to cook, so, shut up—or tonight you won't be eating!"

"Never upset the cook," said Arian, smiling.

Sabino couldn't wait to taste his friend's pasta alla Norma. The day before, luckily, they had found a small house with a nice kitchen only a few yards from the lake.

After all those attempts, I am starving, Sabino thought. He had spent all morning with Arian, trying to make the writing on the papyrus reappear.

Ciccio examined the contents of the bags. "What the heck are these? You call these eggplants? They are small, dried out and colorless. And the pasta...? I said sedani rigati, not rigatoni! What the hell, Arian!"

"Don't look at me. Egil took care of the pasta," she replied, raising her hands.

The Sicilian hit his forehead with the palm of his hand, exclaiming: "But why? You gave the most important job to the person that knows the least about cooking!"

The three were silent.

"Get out! Out of my kitchen before you do any more damage!"

Sabino was about to follow his two friends, but the chef told him to stay. "You stay here and give me a hand."

"But I don't know how to cook."

"You'll learn."

Ciccio gave him a cutting board, the eggplants, and a knife. "Be sure to slice them very thin, but not too thin, lo capisti?"

Sabino nodded, looking at the big utensil. "Did you see this? It looks like a samurai sword!" he said, turning it in his hands. "I think it's dangerous to have something like this in the kitchen. Someone could get hurt!"

"Don't worry, picciò!" Ciccio reassured him, turning the pasta sauce in the pot. "When we finish, that razor-sharp knife will return to its original form: ten harmless spoons."

He smiled in amusement, seeing that Sabino could not get his head around it.

"You didn't understand much, did you?"

"No, not really."

"Let me give you a practical example. Give me one of your rings."

"Be careful, I care about this one!"

Ciccio closed his hand around it. When he reopened it, in its place there was a coin.

"Uagliò! Very, very cool!" Sabino exclaimed, admiringly. "How did you do it? Can you teach me the trick?"

"There is no trick," explained Ciccio. "It is all thanks to my relic. Since the bracelet and I are one, not only can I turn into an animal, but I can also change form and substance of any metal object, lo capisti?"

Sabino began to slice the eggplants. "Wow, this power really has a thousand useful applications," he mused. "Imagine how useful it could be in everyday life! You could fix anything!"

"You are so naïve…" retorted Ciccio, adding salt to the boiling water. "Now I can't stop thinking that I could open locks effortlessly by just turning any metal object into the right key!"

Sabino frowned, puzzled.

"Ironically," Ciccio continued, "now that robbing does not interest me, I wouldn't have any competition. In the beginning, when I was about your age, things were more difficult…"

Sabino was stunned.

"Do you mean to say that…" he whispered without finding the courage to finish the sentence.

"Yes, you got that right, picciò." Ciccio lit a cigarette. "The Corleone family has always supported itself through illegal activities. And I, as a good son, began to make my contribution early on. Under the guidance of my dad, Santuzzo, I began to mug and steal cars. Minchia, if I had had this bracelet then…"

"You would have understood it was time to get back on the right track," said Arian from the door, slightly ajar. "Do not mislead the boy!"

"Fimmena, when I speak about my family, you must show respect, lo capisti?"

Arian vanished. Ciccio seemed relieved.

"Where were we?" he asked Sabino, checking the pasta sauce.

"You were telling me about car thefts…"

"Yes. I soon realized that my hands weren't very good at stealing, so I used them for other things."

"Like embroidery?"

"Ah, are you being funny?" he chuckled, and Sabino was relieved the sharp joke had hit home. "Good! That's how I like you! To tell you the truth, I boxed at an almost professional level. As a result, I was employed as a bodyguard for my big brother, Rosario. We were formidable together. One bad day, however, the Chrismatics arrested us because of a batch of fake relics."

Sabino lost his smile.

Ciccio's voice was grave when he finished, "Rosario, who had the fake relics, took all the blame and was burned at the stake."

A heavy silence fell in the kitchen. For a few instants, Sabino could hear only the pasta sauce bubbling in the pot.

"I am sorry…"

"Don't be," Ciccio said with a false lightness. "Give me the eggplants and the pasta."

"And you? How did you manage?"

Ciccio poured the pasta into the boiling water and said, "Unlike Rosario, I was taken to a place worse than the most terrible hell you could ever imagine: Sancta Sanctorum."

He had a dull look on his face. At that moment, as the rigatoni surfaced from the bottom of the pot, so did his terrible memories.

"I was chained and tortured in the most horrible ways," he continued. "I was shown no mercy. Then, one day, before the usual flagellation, they placed a dog next to me..."

"A dog? Did I understand correctly?"

"Capisti... capisti... You understood just fine. Without an ounce of humanity, they slit that poor beast's throat right in front of me as they pierced my hands and feet... That animal never sinned in its life, and those bastards killed it without mercy. Then I did not feel any more pain, only anger and blind rage..."

His hands were shaking.

"Calm down, Ciccio..." Sabino placed a hand on his shoulder. "Everything is okay..."

The man was getting redder and redder. "I don't know who gave me the strength... I tore the chains and I pounced on those bastards. Then, I don't remember anything else...."

Sabino realized he had backed away from Ciccio as he spoke, until his back was against the door.

"Don't worry," Ciccio said with a smirk. "I am okay now. Come here."

"Are you sure?"

Ciccio's laugh sounded more like a bark. "Of course! And don't forget: never walk away from the stove! Come on, check the pasta."

Sabino tasted it and said: "A few more minutes."

"Good. Set the table and I will deal with the pots."

Nodding, Sabino opened a drawer taking out a checkered tablecloth.

Ciccio sighed. "I am sorry for before. I try to stay calm, but there are some topics that make me lose my temper… The point is that, shortly after, like Egil, an old man called Matusalem of Bari took me to Bishop Grassano, who managed to get me off the street. I realized that on my wrist I had this bracelet. You see, since joining our relics, we have become different, probably better people. My story proves it in an unmistakable way. That is why I told it to you. The relic is not a burden, not at all. It is a blessing. Lo capisti?"

Sabino gave him two thumbs up.

"Okay then, go and get those slackers!" ordered his friend, turning the stove off. Loudly, he added: "The food is ready! Come and eat!"

XIV

"No way!" shouted Sabino, adamant. "I am not doing it!"

He pulled his hood up while his teeth chattered from the cold. The three Martyrs, despite his objections, had dragged him to the summit of a remote mountain.

"Come on, this is our last chance," Egil urged him. "We cannot waste any more time. We need results. And now. That's why we must do it."

"Oh yeah?" Sabino objected. "Is smashing against the rocks below the excellent result we need? Because this is what's going to happen, do you understand?"

"To be precise," Arian interjected, "technically, you would have a better chance to go for a swim in the Garigliano river below, after going through the thick fog than smashing against the rocks… But, as Egil was telling you, you will land safe and sound because the Shroud will protect you."

"Oh yeah?" Sabino countered. "So, since you are so sure I have full control, explain to me why I can't make the writing appear on that crap papyrus!"

"We already told you," replied Arian with a bored expression. "You need to focus on the vocation of your relic. Only then you'll have full control."

"Okay, okay, but this is not a good reason to kill me! There must be less dangerous ways to teach me how to engage my vocation!" replied Sabino.

He was getting angry.

"There are, but they require time," continued Arian, with her lecturing voice. "It took Ciccio several weeks to focus his vocation on instinct, Egil's on duty, and me on…" A bitter smile appeared on her lips. "I am so focused that I get to know things I don't want to."

Sabino rolled his eyes.

Resuming her annoying teacher's tone, she continued. "The Shroud's vocation is protection. And the urge to protect your own life is the strongest urge you can feel. Come on, be reasonable. Trust us: nothing bad will happen to you."

Sabino could no longer take the stupid conversation. He looked below into the ravine once more: an abyss made up of rocks with a milky river and cold fog at its base. The wind howled through the mountain gorges, giving the landscape an even more ghostly appearance.

"Nope, nope, and nope! I won't jump in there for any reason whatsoever. Let's leave!"

Suddenly, two strong hands got a hold of him from behind and lifted him six feet off the ground. It was Ciccio.

"Picciò, you are busting our cugghiùni!"

"No!" shouted Sabino, wiggling like a maniac. "Let me go, Ciccio! Let me go!"

"Absolutely!" his friend replied, hurling him into the ravine.

The wind lashed Sabino's body. Soon the mist engulfed him.

As his screams died in his throat, he focused on the relic.

Save me, Shroud! he thought, his heart racing. *You are the only one that can help me!*

The world around him was spinning madly.

Shroud, help me! he prayed as he was sucked into a spiral of trees, rocks, and sky. *I don't want to die!*

"Fuck!" Sabino mumbled, gagging. He had started to vomit as soon as he touched the ground. Ciccio, as the eagle, had rescued him when he had fainted.

He tried to get back on his feet, but his stomach made him gag again.

After a couple of disgusting minutes, Sabino stopped throwing up. Once he stood, he spewed all his anger, fists shaking at his sides. "You, sons of bitches! I told you it wouldn't work! And stupid me for trusting you!"

Ignoring him, Egil walked over to Arian, who was silently looking at the landscape, standing by the edge of the cliff.

"We don't have any more time to try," he told her, disappointed. "Let's go to Naples and let's hope the Bishop can help us."

Sabino was still very angry. "Hey, you, dickheads, I am talking to you! Don't play dumb! What happened to all your talks about trust? Is this how you treat your friends?"

"Amunìnne, picciò!" Ciccio exclaimed, slapping him on the shoulder. "Don't be upset. Come and piss with me. You know that if you don't piss in good company..."

"Fuck pissing!" blurted out Sabino. "You can all go fuck yourselves! You and your fucking methods."

Giggling, Ciccio walked past him, heading for the woods, which made Sabino even angrier.

"Damn it!" he shouted, kicking a stone with all his strength. "As of now, I am done with you! I am leaving! I really want to see who is going to save your asses next time!"

It was then that Arian turned toward him. Even though he could not see her eyes, as they were protected by the sunglasses, as always, he felt her stare piercing his soul.

"Only you can save me now," she said to him.

Two incredulous sets of eyes saw the woman fold her arms and jump into the ravine.

"What the fuck?" railed Egil.

Sabino rushed to the edge of the cliff in time to see Arian disappear into the mist.

"Where's Ciccio?" asked Egil, looking around in a frenzy.

"Ciccio!" shouted Sabino. "Hurry, come here, Arian just jumped!"

Ciccio's voice made its way to them through the woods: "Great! One less problem!"

"Shit!"

Egil ran toward the voice, leaving Sabino alone.

The boy thought he was going crazy.

Egil and Ciccio would never make it.

He inhaled deeply and then leapt, once more plummeting into the void.

Come on Shroud! he thought as he fell at a crazy speed. *This time I am not asking for myself… Do it for Arian! Help me save her!*

The bandana lit up with the whitest white.

"Yes! Arian, wait for us! We are coming!"

The light enveloped Sabino, who shone like a comet launched at an incredible speed. He wasn't afraid; he was only apprehensive about the fate of his… How should he define her? Yes, that's it—his *friend*.

He darted through the mist, and in the blink of an eye, he was next to her. Soon, the glowing halo expanded, becoming a sphere to contain them both. They fluctuated in midair, only a few feet above the river.

Straddling the curve at the base of the sphere of light, the two found themselves on top of each other.

"Arian, are you okay?"

"It seems so," coughed the woman, getting up with difficulty.

"That's great!" Sabino sighed, hugging her.

A moment later he withdrew, embarrassed.

"Where are you going?" Arian called him back. "I am not going to eat you!"

Heartened, Sabino hugged her again, happy. In the meantime, the glowing sphere had brought them back gently to the top.

"Damn you!" cried Ciccio, puffing smoke, to Arian. "What the minchia were you thinking?"

"Guys, I figured it all out!" she surprised them. "No wonder we were unsuccessful. We were pushing Sabino on the wrong vocation!"

"I told you so!" gloated Sabino. "DJ S.P. is never wrong! You almost had me on your conscience!"

Egil was distraught: "Why such a crazy act? Have you gone crazy?"

Arian crossed her arms with a grin of satisfaction. "Not at all. The Shroud's vocation is not protection, as we thought, but sacrificio."

Sabino could not believe his ears.

"Sacrificio…" said Egil. "To save others at the expense of yourself…"

"Every time the Shroud has granted me powers was, mostly, to save you guys," Sabino reflected.

Arian smiled at him. "It also did it because every time you were ready to give all of yourself for us. And that is no small thing, you know?"

Sabino had never thought of himself as a selfless person. Could this be one of the effects of the relic, as Ciccio mentioned to him? Or had he always been this way, and he never had the courage to admit it?

"Either way, Arian," he replied, a bit embarrassed. "Don't you ever do such a thing again, ok? I feel like I lost ten years of my life from the scare."

"I am sorry, but I will keep on doing it."

Her answer shocked him.

"Mine wasn't a 'crazy gesture,'" she continued, "but a gesture of faith. And it is thanks to my faith in you that you now know how to use your relic, finally."

Suddenly, Sabino felt ashamed to have doubted his fellow Martyrs. Despite appearances, they had shown they were ready to die for him. It made him feel both proud and safe. As if they were a family.

"Thank you so much! I believe I finally learned how to master my relic. Where is the papyrus?"

He felt ready to face the whole world.

"In the car!" Egil urged them. "Let's do everything in the car! If we don't leave immediately, the Chrismatics will get to the Bishop in Naples before us."

Without further ado, the four Martyrs rushed to the car.

"Let's wait until we are done with the turns," said Arian. "I hate reading in the car, let alone around curves!"

XV

Arian unrolled the papyrus in the middle of the back seat. "Your turn, Sabino. I can't wait to read it!"

Between Egil's glances in the rearview mirror and Ciccio's feigned nonchalance, it was hard for Sabino not to feel anxious. Everyone expected great things from him. He inhaled deeply and closed his eyes.

Dear Shroud, he thought, *I need your help. Let us read this message. Not only because this way you and I aren't going to look stupid, but mostly because this message's content can save the world…*

"It's working!"

Arian's excitement stopped his train of thought in its tracks.

Opening his eyes, Sabino saw the bandana glowing, while on the papyrus, those strange, incomprehensible symbols appeared again.

"You rock!" Egil cheered, giving Sabino a thumb up.

"'I, Paolo Amico, servant of God, of Christ, and the Apostle of Blessed Joseph of Arimathea,'" Arian began to read. Her voice was solemn.

"And who the minchia is Paolo Amico?" demanded Ciccio, showing how distracted he had been at the convent.

"If I remember correctly," replied Arian, restating what the abbess had told them, "the tradition of Joseph's Apostles records him as one of the most authoritative and important figures in early Christianity."

Sabino was consumed by nervousness. "Sorry guys, let's leave the questions for later and read the entire text first. You never know…"

"I concur," said Arian, resuming her ciphering. "Listen to how the text continues: '…Apostle of Blessed Joseph of Arimathea and custodian of the Holy Grail, I write these words inspired by the vision of the Almighty…'"

Then Arian spent interminable minutes talking to herself. In his heart, Sabino prayed for the Shroud to continue assisting him. For the common good, of course. Impressing Arian never entered his mind.

"'On this day,'" Arian resumed, "'October 31, 1239 in the Year of Our Lord, the Lord has manifested Himself to me in the small chapel of Santa Maria del Monte, near the hamlet of Andria in Puglia. It is here, the Almighty told me, that you will place the Grail. It will remain there until the right moment. And so I did…'"

"Santa Maria del Monte?" Egil asked, confused.

"Don't stop," Sabino told Arian, cutting Egil short. "What else does it say?"

"Nothing," Arian said hesitantly. "The papyrus ends there. The rest might be written on the parchment kept in Naples."

"So…we did it?" he asked.

"Yes, we did!" answered Arian beaming. "Congratulations, I am proud of you."

Ciccio shook his head. "Explain to me one thing: in the area surrounding Andria there must be at least a hundred churches. Am I wrong or is this papyrus useful as a minchia?"

Sabino groaned. "Thanks a lot! I bend backward to make you read those symbols and this is the thank you I get?"

Egil chuckled in the rearview mirror.

"Santa Maria del Monte…" Arian muttered. "Where have I heard that name before?"

"We'll ask Bishop Centritto," said Egil. "Naples, here we come!"

"Just wait a minute!" Ciccio barked, his tone surprising the other passengers. Then, he softened. "If you all agree, from today we can consider Sabino a Martyr, just like us."

Sabino looked down at his feet. "Like you? Nah, let's not be silly…"

"Right!" Egil said, ignoring Sabino's protests. "Today is a very important day for you, and to end it on a high note, you will go through the ritual…"

"The ritual?" Sabino repeated, butterflies swarming his stomach. "What is it about?"

"It is a very ancient tradition passed down by the followers of Joseph of Arimathea, amico."

"So, what will I have to do?" He glanced between Egil and Ciccio. "And aren't we in a rush?"

Ciccio cast knowing glances at the other two. "It won't take long."

The car left the road and drove through brushwood until it came near a small stream. The four friends got out and walked toward the bank. An icy wind was blowing from the north.

Ciccio lit a cigarette. "Okay, Sabino…get undressed!"

Sabino hugged his shoulders, embarrassed. "Um…I don't understand. Weren't we supposed to fish?"

"Oh, come on!" Egil prodded impatiently. "You just need to get undressed, get into the water, and stay there until the end of the ritual. Hurry up; we can't stay here until dawn!"

Sabino obeyed, blushing more and more, until he was left only in his underwear.

"Those, of course, you can keep," said Arian, to Sabino's relief. "Now get into the water and kneel."

Sabino cast a pleading look in Ciccio's direction.

The Sicilian picked up Sabino's hoodie, moving it from one hand to the other, completely unaware of Sabino's wish for help. "The writing 'E.G.' on your hoodie—what minchia does it mean? 'Ero giovane—I was young'?"

Shaking from the cold, Sabino replied, "No! 'E.G.' is Estrema Guardia. It's the name of a group a lot of my friends belong to."

"Estrema Guardia—Extreme Guard? Oh come on now… What kind of fans are those?" Egil asked, grabbing Sabino by an arm and flinging him into the creek. "Enough chit-chatting! Arian, since Bishop Grassano is not here, you officiate the ritual. You are the oldest."

Arian approached slowly, as though she was concerned Egil's antics might splash her. "I want to clarify that the title of oldest is not because of age but because I was the first to perform a miracle…"

"Okay, okay, I got it!" Sabino's teeth chattered. "Hurry up! I am freezing!"

"In nomine Patris et Filii et Spiritus Sancti..." Arian made the sign of the cross, echoed by the others. "Today the power of the holy relic consubstantiated in you has fully manifested..."

She poured water from the stream on Sabino's head, who let a few silent swearwords slip out.

"Swearing is not welcome," Arian pointed out.

Ciccio chuckled and cast a knowing glance at Egil.

"As of today, you are a new person," she continued. "Sabino Pignataro, from this moment on, you will be known by a new name among the followers of Joseph."

Again, she poured cold water on his head. A shiver ran down his back.

"Pick a new name! One that identifies you as a follower. Choose it using the letters of your own name, but it needs to be new, a symbol of your new life..."

Almost frozen, he called out, "I choose the name Sabi!"

Arian burst out laughing and splashed him again: "Sabi? Too common place. It's not a Martyr's name at all... Pick another one!"

"Pigna!"

"What? Are you kidding?" Egil scolded him, using a tone that would have convinced anyone. "That sucks big time!"

Once again, water ran down Sabino's head.

"Saro!" he shouted, teeth still chattering.

It was Ciccio's turn. "I'll be happy…when you will tell me your next choice. This one just doesn't work!"

The icy wind howled powerfully.

Sabino, freezing, tried one last time: "Taro!"

Arian seemed uncertain. "Not bad… Guys, what do you say?"

"Well, I don't know…" said Egil stepping forward.

Cicio followed suit. "Taro could work but…"

Without any warning Arian began splashing their new Martyr, and Egil and Ciccio did the same.

"You sons of…" cursed Sabino, responding as best he could to the waves coming from everywhere. After a few minutes of splashing, shoving, and cursing, the other Martyrs retreated, laughing.

"Well, Taro," concluded Arian, fixing her sunglasses on her nose. "The ritual is finished. Welcome among us!"

"What a fucked-up welcome!" retorted Sabino, sneezing. "Nice ritual, really! You gave me a shitty name and I am almost certain I caught pneumonia."

"Minchia, Sabì, you should have seen your face!" commented Ciccio. "You were really a minchione, idiot! You chose your name yourself, like we all did!"

"Come on, boys!" said Egil, already in the driver's seat. "Let's go. Naples is waiting for us!"

"You are such a bore, yankee!" complained Ciccio. "Let us have some more fun!"

Arian got into the car with a sigh. "I am afraid the time for fun is over…"

XVI

Naples, Episcopal Curia

The front door vibrated with heavy blows. Outside, someone was anxious to get in.

"Wait, mo' vengo… I am coming… Marònna d'o Carmine—what is it? Has o' Vesuvio blown up?"

A small window opened.

"We are from the Annularia brotherhood," Arian announced. "We urgently need to speak with Bishop Centritto…"

"But che, pazziamm'—are you crazy? Come back tomorrow! The bishop is sleeping," replied an elderly voice.

"Sorry to insist," continued Arian, "but His Most Excellent Holiness would be mad with both us and you if we don't get to speak with the bishop. We have to share extremely important information."

"What? The patriarch? San Gennario mio! Oh my, oh my," exclaimed the old man. "Wait a minute, I am going to wake up the bishop."

He then closed the window, and after a few minutes of silence, the front door opened.

"Excuse the wait," the man apologized. "The bishop will see you very soon. Please, come in."

Sabino, now Taro, followed his companions into a large hall with frescoed walls. The paintings depicted scenes from the saints' lives; in the room there were also two prie-dieu, a sofa, and a couch. It was the perfect waiting room of a holy place.

"My name is Massimo, your servant," the elderly man introduced himself once the four sat down. "Would you like me to prepare you something? I make a mean coffee. And I also have two warm sfogliatelle…"

"Thanks, but no," Egil cut him short. "We just want to see the bishop."

"Yes, be patient a bit longer. He is getting dressed. Anyway, I have never seen pilgrims like you before… I understand you are American, right? I have been to New York, when a was a guaglione, a boy, and I could even speak a little bit of English…"

"My mother was from Dallas, Texas," answered Egil proudly. "My father, on the other hand, was from Genoa. In any case, even though I am a dual citizen, I feel very Italian."

"That does you credit," Arian interrupted him, visibly displeased. "We are all coming from Trapani. We've had quite the journey, didn't we, Francesco?"

She elbowed Ciccio.

"From Trapani? Absolutely! Minchia, what a trip we had… I'm beat."

Taro, meanwhile, studied the frescoes on the walls until the sound of a bell in the distance drew his attention.

"Ah, the bishop is ready," Massimo announced. "If you would like to follow me. Please, this way."

The four Martyrs got up and walked down the well-lit hall. At the end stood two big white doors. Massimo knocked at the door on the right and opened it, peeking inside.

"Your Excellency, the Annularia delegation is here," he announced in a whisper.

"Let them in," replied a deep, hoarse voice.

Massimo stepped aside closing the door behind them.

Taro stood speechless. The large room opened onto a magnificent hall; the light marble floor was covered in floral decorations displaying immaculate details. On the walls, dozens of wooden shelves overflowed with precisely sorted books, as if no one had consulted them in centuries.

"Sit down, my friends."

Behind a large desk, a Nordic-looking man stood up. His damask chamber robe matched his red hair. A frame of tiny wrinkles embellished his eyes, enlivened by a spray of freckles.

"I am curious to know the reason for which you are bothering me at such a late hour," said the bishop, approaching them circumspectly.

"We are the Martyrs trained by Bishop Grassano," Egil explained, showing his pendant of the cross with the dragon around it. The others did the same, taking out their relics.

Centritto's face relaxed. "Heaven be praised! You are alive!"

"In the flesh!" Ciccio exclaimed. "Would you like a cigarette?"

"Ciccio, please!" Arian rebuked him. Then, addressing the bishop, she asked: "You do know why we are here, right?"

"I believe so," Bishop Centritto told them, sitting down again. "You read the first fragment of the Acts, didn't you?"

"Yes, we did," confirmed Egil. "It said that the Grail is kept in the Church of Santa Maria del Monte, near Andria. None of us, including the Abbess Cinzia, knows where that is."

"By the way, how is Cinzia?" The old bishop's face grew grave with concern. "The newspapers say that her body hasn't been recovered yet. I hope she was able to save herself."

"She is fine," said Taro, smiling. "We left her near Cascia."

"And who might you be?" asked Centritto, who only now seemed to have noticed him. "I was told of only three Martyrs…"

"My name is Sabino—well, it was, but now I am Taro. I am Bishop Alessandro Bafunno's nephew."

"I see." Centritto gestured to the room around them. "If you want, you can stay here with me. I will hide you. Staying with the Martyrs is very dangerous."

"Actually," said Egil, "he is the one who consubstantiated with the Shroud. He is one of us now."

The bishop's eyes lit up. "The ways of the Lord are truly infinite!"

"I am sorry," said Arian, "but we are really in a rush. We'd better get to the point. Even if they think we are dead, one never knows…"

The man got up and reached a marble slab on the floor. It had a detailed daisy, as decorative as an illuminated medieval manuscript, on it. "Come on, give me a hand."

He knelt and inserted his ring into a small recess, barely visible at the center of the flower's corolla. After a quick twisting motion of his wrist, the slab lifted slightly with a dull sound. Egil and Ciccio moved it to the side. Underneath was a big wooden casket with luxurious gold trimmings. Once again, Taro gasped.

"The second fragment of the Acts is here," explained the man, moved. "Let's take it out, but gently."

With extreme caution, the box was lifted and laid on the floor. The lid was immediately opened.

"No… This cannot be," Centritto stammered.

"Minchia! Where is the manuscript?"

"Damn!" Egil cursed. "Someone stole it!"

The chest, lined with pitch-black cloth, was empty.

Taro shook his head. A part of him felt his friend was wrong. "It is here. I can't explain but I feel its presence."

As he spoke the words, the bandana on his forearm began to glow with a faint white light.

"You're right!" confirmed Arian. "It is in the lid."

"In the lid?" the bishop repeated, confused. "I don't see anything! And there are no hidden bottoms!"

They all turned to look at Taro, waiting in suspense. The newly minted Martyr closed his eyes to concentrate.

"I have to make it…"

Slowly, he stretched out his left arm.

"I can do it…"

The bandana around his wrist glowed brighter.

"I want to make it…"

He opened his eyes. Under the astonished stare of all present, even the chest had lit up: it seemed to have taken on an unreal, otherworldly texture.

"I am doing it!"

A brilliant white sphere came out of the lid and floated slowly to Taro's open hand. Gradually, the light dimmed, revealing an ancient manuscript.

"Uagliò, so' fort'!" Taro said proudly, curling the arm that bore the Shroud to show off his bicep.

"Not bad, picciò," admitted Ciccio, grinning as he lit a cigarette. "But you still have some way to go…"

Taro gave the manuscript to Arian, who laid it on the desk, opening it. Everyone gathered around her.

"This seems more understandable," Taro observed. "It looks like Italian, even though the handwriting is crappy."

"It is Medieval Latin," explained Arian with irritation. "But you're right, this text is much clearer than many others I've deciphered. Now, however, I need some quiet time to work."

The four men looked at each other and decided it was better to let her be.

"Have a seat, brave Martyrs." Bishop Centritto walked over to the couches in the room. "I imagine you must be tired."

"Your Excellency, please," said Egil, "could you refrain from calling us Martyrs? I associate this word with suffering and horrible tortures I would prefer not to experience."

"Vero è—so true!" interjected Ciccio. "I have always thought that, too. Your Excellency, who had the idea to call us that?"

The bishop smiled and explained: "Well…it was Alessandro's idea…"

"My uncle?" Taro asked, then chuckled. "I should have suspected it."

"Your uncle," Centritto confirmed. "He suggested the name Martyr to differentiate between consubstantiated Saints from those who are transubstantiated instead," Centritto continued.

"Transubwhat?"

"These are two concepts that are a bit difficult to explain… but if you can give me more of your attention than your uncle told me you paid in school, I can make it clear to you," he concluded.

Taro dipped his head in embarrassment, but he was too eager to learn to be dissuaded. "I'm ready!"

"The starting point are the holy relics," Centritto began. "You know what I'm talking about, right?"

"Yes! The relics are the remains of the saints and retain their powers," Taro recited, pleased he wasn't behind the curve. "Some among them turned again into flesh-and-blood Saints. It was thanks to them we were able to stop the invasion of the Luciferals."

"Yes," Centritto said hesitantly, tilting his head, "more or less. Also, the holy oil that comes out of some of these relics is used by the patriarch to create the Chrismatics through the rite of the Supreme Anointing."

"The holy relics are indestructible, right?" Egin added.

"That's right!" confirmed the bishop. "The most important proof of the sanctity of a holy relic is its absolute incorruptibility."

"So far so good," said Taro.

"Now we go deep into the subject matter," continued the bishop. "Have you ever asked yourself how Saints are reborn?"

"Well, it is a miracle, isn't it? I have always known that one should not ask why miracles happen… We should only thank God when they do."

Centritto sighed. "I also thought that, but when I was transferred to Sancta Sanctorum, I came to know many things that perhaps I should have never known…"

"Hey, wait a minute! Can you tell me what this Sancta Sanctorum is?" Taro turned to his friend. "You also mentioned it, Ciccio."

"Sancta Sanctorum is the name of the secret place where the holy relics become Saints thanks to the faith and the sacrifice of the Hostiae," explained the bishop, as Ciccio's expression darkened.

"The Hostiae are believers, selected among the most faithful and devoted to the Church Dei Invicti Operae, who decided to give their lives for the fight against the Luciferals and are secretly transferred to Sancta Sanctorum. There, each Hostia is assigned a relic and prays to God that he may revive its Saint."

Taro followed the explanation with a mix of awe and curiosity.

"Beside praying, the Hostiae ask to be subjected to the same suffering their saints experienced: whippings, amputations, and afflictions of every kind. They believe this will help them succeed in the Saint's rebirth."

"So, every Saint is reborn from the voluntary sacrifice of a human being?" asked Taro, worried.

"I wish it were only one," replied the bishop with a sad smile. "On average, only one Hostia in every hundred succeeds in reviving a Saint. All the others die, albeit voluntarily, amid prayers and torment."

Taro shuddered. "What happens to those who are successful and revive a Saint?"

"Nothing remains of them. They immolate their body and soul to merge with the holy relic and revive the Saint in exact the same way as they were in their prime. Of the Hostia, only their clothes remain. This is the miracle of transubstantiation."

Egil shook his head. "Is there really no other way to get the Saints reborn?"

"Not until today," the bishop said mysteriously. "By the patriarch's decree, Bishop Boenzi had begun attempts at transubstantiation of the Reiecti, aimed at finding a way to limit the losses of the Hostiae."

"Reiecti?" Ciccio was beginning to get excited. "Minchia, don't tell me that you..."

"I'm so sorry for his choice, my son," Centritto apologized immediately on behalf of Boenzi.

"Figghiu di puttana!" Ciccio stood up shouting, the apology going unheard. "Son of a bitch! I am going to kill you!"

Egil stopped him just in time: long fangs had begun to protrude from his lips and sharp claws from his fingers.

"Stop!" Egil shouted. "It wasn't him! Bishop Boenzi is dead, do you remember or not? Stop!"

Taro sat, frozen by fear. He watched as the beast slowly regained the appearance of his friend.

"It might be better to change the subject," ended the bishop.

"No, go ahead," said Ciccio, his hands shaking as he lit another cigarette. "I let it all out."

Centritto watched him a moment longer, lips pursed, before turning back to Taro. "Simply put, the Reiecti are criminals sentenced to death and destined for Sancta Sanctorum. They were used like guinea pigs: all kinds of experiments were performed on them that might facilitate transubstantiation, in order to spare the precious Hostiae."

"All of this is atrocious!" Taro observed indignantly.

"Yes," admitted the bishop. "Apart from Ciccio's case, which has been archived in the records of Sancta Santorum as 'not received,' none of our attempts with the Reiecti were successful. For this reason, Bishop Boenzi asked the patriarch to suspend their use."

"I can already imagine the answer," Ciccio said bitterly.

Centritto sighed, unable to argue. "So, to sum up, transubstantiation is the miracle that allows a very determined volunteer to merge with a holy relic. The achieved result is to revive the Saint to whom the holy relics belonged. Is it all clear so far?"

Taro nodded.

"That's the Saints. Now let's talk about you, Martyrs. The starting points for both are always the holy relics. In them is contained not only the power but also the conscience and the personality of the saint. They are not to be considered simple objects, but real persons. They contain the soul of the saint, which observes and judges us at every moment. In some extremely rare cases, the saint can decide to interact with the outside world, producing miracles as consubstantiation."

"Meaning?"

"The soul of the saint contained in the relic decides to assist a human being and takes on a new form that allows it to bond with the chosen one, who acquires the ability to work wonders."

Taro twisted his arm, looking at the white cloth around him. "But how come the Shroud chose me?"

"Minchia, good question!" Ciccio snorted, putting out his cigarette in a crystal ashtray.

"If we know very little about transubstantiation," replied the bishop, "about consubstantiation, we know even less. The two most likely hypotheses are affinity and faith. According to Abbess Cinzia, the holy relics choose whom to unite with depending on the affinity they feel they have with the person or the situation they are experiencing. For example, Egil was mortally wounded in the very place where Saint George became a martyr, and he remained faithful to his ideals just as the saint did, in his time, when dying. Something similar must have happened between Saint Francis and Ciccio, Saint Lucia and Arian, the Shroud and you."

"I understand," said Taro looking at the bandana on his arm. It hadn't been there long, but he felt it was his, as if he had it all along.

"As far as faith is concerned, I don't believe I need to explain. To conclude, Alessandro decided to identify you as Martyrs because you have been and continue to be living witnesses of the miracle of consubstantiation."

"Done!" Arian announced. "I finished translating."

"Minchia, you took your time," Ciccio teased her.

"So, what does the papyrus say?" asked Egil impatiently.

"It is written by one Father Mario Lanza, who claims to be a disciple of Paolo Amico."

Making the sign of the cross, Bishop Centritto observed, "It is a great honor to be able to read the writings of two such distinguished fathers."

"I am going to translate the most important part," Arian continued. "'God has inspired my trembling hand right here in the fortified sanctuary where the Holy Grail is hidden…'"

"That's great!" exclaimed Ciccio. "But wasn't the Holy Grail in a church? From what you've just read, it's in a fortress! Or am I wrong?"

The bishop sat behind his desk and turned on his computer. "Let's proceed in order. What did you say the church was called?"

"Santa Maria del Monte," Arian replied. "It should be around Andria, in Puglia."

"Let's check the database."

The blue light from the screen illuminated the bishop's face as he typed on the keyboard. "Unbelievable…" he muttered suddenly. "Look what we found!"

The four Martyrs went around the desk and stood behind the bishop. An expression of incredulous wonder formed on Taro's face. A picture of an ancient octagonal building towering over the top of a hill filled the screen: eight towers were arranged at the corners, giving the whole building the form of a huge crown.

"It's Castel del Monte!" exclaimed Arian. "So much for a church!"

"But are we sure?" asked Ciccio.

"According to the database," replied the Bishop, "the castle was built right where the church of Santa Maria del Monte stood. The church no longer exists today."

"I'll finish translating the text for you," Arian said, eager to find a solution to the riddle. "Although the part that comes now is the least clear."

Everyone shifted next to her, to the side of the desk where the ancient manuscript lay open.

"'He who will seek communion with the Holy Grail must follow the path taken by Christ.'"

"Taro, since the Shroud chose you," Centritto intervened, "by the principle of affinity—of which we have spoken before—it is very likely that the Grail will also accept communion with you."

"So, what should I do to follow Christ's example? Grow a beard and hair?"

"You're such a minchione!" Ciccio gave him a slap on the back of the head.

"I can already see you," Egil added, "with twelve apostles following you. Can we go with you, master?"

Barely holding back laughter, Taro assumed a blessing pose. "I will make you into a guide of souls."

Everyone burst into thunderous laughter, with the exception of Arian.

"Come on!" she blurted out. "Can you just stop? Or do we want to spend the night telling jokes?"

"All jokes aside, are there any other interesting things written there?" asked Egil, recovering his usual serious tone.

"Unfortunately, no. Only prayers and orations."

"Well, then let's go."

"Wait a moment," the bishop interrupted them. "I have one thing to ask you."

"What is it?" the woman asked.

"More than a request, it is a prayer. Taro, I am asking you on behalf of all the members of the Hand of God..."

The boy was stunned. Solemn speeches made him always a little uncomfortable.

"We hope that you will reach Apotheosis. Believe in your comrades and especially in yourself. Use the power of the Grail to preserve humanity, however sinful it may be. Only then will we be able to stop the forthcoming Armageddon the patriarch is preparing. Do not make the same mistake he did, launching into a war that would only lead to the destruction of us, human beings."

"I will," replied Taro, his eyes full of emotion and his heart in turmoil.

"Have faith and nothing will stop you," the bishop concluded.

The Martyrs bid him farewell and left the large room. Halfway down the hall, they met Maximus.

"Well?" the old man asked. "How did it go? Shall I make you some coffee?"

"No, thank you," replied Arian. "You are really too kind."

"That's the least I can do. Shall I prepare the guest room for you? You must be dead tired."

"Not at all," Egil replied, wryly. "The night is young! Now we are going to the disco!"

"Lucky you!" sighed Maximus. There was something strange in his eyes, but Taro told himself that strange impression must depend on his own tiredness.

The old man, having reached the end of the corridor, opened the front door.

"Until next time, then!" he dismissed them, with a broad smile.

In his study, the bishop was absorbed in analyzing the manuscript. With a large magnifying glass, he meticulously examined its inscriptions, enraptured by the skilled handwriting.

After jotting down a few words, he pulled a digital camera from a desk drawer and began to capture the precious find. But suddenly, the door swung open.

"Damn it, Maximus! How many times have I told you that you must knock before entering?"

"Monsignor Centritto, you are under arrest."

The voice didn't belong at all to the old man. The bishop lifted his head and saw a dozen Chrismatics enter his room with spears and drawn swords. Up front, one of them, covered in golden armor, swaggered forward.

"Captain Altamura, how dare you enter my study this way? I demand an explanation now!" the bishop ordered.

"The charges against you are heresy, first and foremost, as well as aiding and abetting criminals," clarified the captain. "Follow me to the cathedral without resistance."

"What are you talking about?" protested the bishop as two Chrismatics handcuffed him. "You know me. You know what I'm made of!"

"The CCTV footage is unequivocal. We never expected this from you," Altamura confessed, unflinching.

Centritto was distraught. As he was being led away, his eyes raced to the small camera set high on the ceiling. A red light, almost imperceptible, revealed that it was still on.

Standing at the main entrance, Maximus clasped his arms around his body, his face mortified.

"I'm sorry, Your Excellency," he said, in tears. "If I hadn't recorded everything, they would have jailed us both! I have a family!"

"God sees and provides," replied the bishop, gravely. "I am sure He will be able to forgive you."

XVII

A16 Highway, Thursday, November 1st
Celebration of All Saints, United in Glory with Christ

The full moon, high in the sky, made the slopes of Mount Vesuvius, which could be seen in the distance, sparkle with silvery reflections. The headlights of the SUV lit the semi-deserted lane and Taro, who was driving, felt like a king.

"Feel the power of this thing! It really is a beast of a car!" he exclaimed, excited.

"And this is nothing," pointed out Egil, who was sitting next to him. "You should have seen the jeeps I used to take to the desert!"

"How many gears does it have? Weren't five enough?"

"Listen, rookie," Ciccio said, "enjoy the moment, because after the next gas station, I will be the one driving."

"Hey, that isn't fair!" Taro pouted. "You promised me I would drive!"

"Yes, but I didn't promise that you would drive all the way to the castle… Besides, sitting in the back here with Arian—I am so bored!"

Arian completely ignored his words.

"That's not the way it works," protested Taro. "A promise is a promise. So, next stop: Castel del Monte!"

"Well, now that I think of it, I feel like driving," interjected Egil.

Suddenly, the car was hit by a series of vibrations of increasing intensity.

The ground was shaking.

"Hold on tight!" Taro shouted as he tried to maintain control of the car.

Terrible tremors shook the road; the asphalt had already begun to crack. Listening to his gut, Taro hit the brakes. The car spun several times as boiling vapors surfaced from the cracks in the road. Finally, the car came to a halt, and about one hundred feet in front of them, a huge hole appeared; red sparks of glowing lava oozed out and into the street.

Due to the tremors, the SUV was shaking so violently that it would soon tip over. Taro felt he was about to faint.

"Everyone out!" ordered Egil.

Everyone responded except for Taro, who realized that terror was keeping him from moving.

Egil rushed to undo his seatbelt, taking Taro in his arms and out of the car.

"My God! Taro!" shouted Arian, running toward them.

"There will never be salvation for those who turn their backs on the Light!"

The voice, clear and mighty, overpowered every other noise. In front of our four Martyrs appeared a man in his thirties, wearing white clothing partially covered by a scarlet red cloak. On his head sat a golden tiara with a Latin cross in the middle. In his left hand he was clutching a carved crosier.

"Followers of the Anti-Christ!" he called them as the ground kept on shaking. "I, Gennaro, protector of the city of Naples, will stop your mission!"

Taro, in his friend's arms, was feeling weaker and weaker. He was certain he was about to lose consciousness.

"You take care of him!" said Arian to Egil. "We will take care of this one!"

On ground shaken by tremors, the Saint walked toward them with outstretched arms.

"Abandon your foolish intents! Turn and admire the Light, or you will sink into darkness!"

"Minchia! If there is one thing I can't stand is the self-righteous talk," Ciccio commented, crouching on the ground. An emerald green light enveloped him completely.

Arian aimed her guns at their enemy.

"Do not take another step, or I'll place two holes in your forehead!" she warned the Saint.

A powerful roar made her threat even more fearsome. Next to her, where Ciccio had been, now stood a huge black panther. Taro found enough strength to smile. His friends would protect him. Egil put him down to don his armor.

"Why are you refusing salvation?" asked Gennaro.

Suddenly, the earthquake stopped. The adversaries stared at one another in total silence as the peak of Mount Vesuvius glowed with reddish sparks. Taro's heart raced in his chest.

"Forgive them, Lord. They do not know what they are doing! Burning abyss, welcome them in your purifying embrace!" uttered the Saint, grasping the crosier with both hands and driving it hard into the asphalt.

The ground resumed shaking with newly found violence, and a network of cracks filled with lava opened all around. A crackling opening spread very quickly from the crosier toward the Martyrs. Taro shouted, and Egil took him back in his arms. Arian and the panther immediately jumped to the side as Egil's shining greaves sank into a pool of lava that had suddenly appeared.

"Die, you bastard!" shouted Arian, shooting plumbeum bullets wildly.

Riddled with dozens of rounds, Gennaro staggered. The instant the two empty magazines hit the ground rattling, the panther pounced on the Saint and sank its jaws in his throat, swallowing his blood and battering his body with his sharp claws. It was only then that the ground stopped shaking.

"Hurry, Arian!" shouted Egil, as the lava was now reaching his knees. "Take Taro!"

The boy's field of vision began to fill with black dots.

"But you…" Arian mumbled, confused, leaning toward him.

"Don't worry about me. My holy armor protects me even though I can't move my legs. *Come on,* save him!"

Arian grabbed Taro, who was mumbling meaningless words.

"Hang on, Egil!" shouted Ciccio, returning to human form. He approached the lava pool, ready to save his comrade. Drenched in sweat, he unbuttoned his shirt collar and loosened the knot in his tie.

"Hey, what the fuck is going on?"

Taro, in Egil and Arian's arms, was paralyzed. It wasn't terror that had made him like that but a supernatural force.

"Shit!" cursed Egil. "I can't move!"

Arian tried to pull her friend closer to her. She was also unable to control her own body.

"Don't worry, my friends," Ciccio sighed. "I'll save you!"

When he reached the puddle, his knees gave out suddenly. Dark smoke vented from his nostrils and ears.

The earth resumed shaking violently. Huge cracks appeared on the road as Gennaro's body began to shine with a golden light. Slowly, he got to his feet, unharmed. The plumbeum bullets that had hit him slid down his robes, clinking at his feet.

"Blasphemous Anti-Christ, not even the most powerful of your demonic alchemy will be able to extinguish the light of true faith," he said, walking toward the crosier stuck in the asphalt.

Taro felt lucid again. "Let's stop this once and for all! I am not the Anti-Christ, and we are not your enemies!"

"Since the world began, no liar has ever admitted to lying," Gennaro said serenely. "You won't fool me, Anti-Christ!"

Taro looked around, trying to assess the situation. They were about to sink into the lava, and none of them would be able to avoid it.

This can't be the end, he thought. *I have to do something. But what? I must have faith... Yes, I must have faith!*

"Goodbye, devil's servants," the Saint bid them smugly. "The scorching abyss will purify your sins."

He stuck his crosier even deeper into the asphalt. At that moment, Taro's bandana began to shine. With a jerk, Arian bent backward, releasing all her accumulated muscular tension, and ended up on the ground with him. Panting from the effort, the two saw Egil sink into a whirlpool of lava. The boy immediately rushed to the pool of searing magma, stretching out his arms. He was hit by the unbearable heat, but he still managed to grab his friend's gloved hand and stuck his feet deep in the ground so he wouldn't also sink.

"Your fate is sealed," continued Gennaro, pushing his crosier deeper into the ground.

The lava vortex swirled dangerously. Heavy fumes rose from the pool, and Taro began to cough violently.

"Let me go and run!" shouted Egil, now submerged in the puddle up to his neck.

"No! I am not leaving without you!"

"Have faith!"

With a quick gesture, Egil slipped his hand out of his armored glove, and Taro fell to the ground as the lava moved closer to his feet. In the horrible instant, the fiery magma melted the flesh and bones of Egil's hand before swallowing the entire Martyr.

Taro shouted until his throat felt on fire.

"Do not despair," said Gennaro, taking his crosier out of the asphalt. "Soon you will be together again...in Hell!"

"If this is the way it has to be," said Arian, sniffling. "Show us the way."

With the swiftness of lighting, she fired again and again at the enemy, but the bullets bounced off his robes like rubber balls off granite.

"Plumbeum again? My miraculous blood is now immune to your cheap alchemy."

Taro stood up and, drying his tears, slipped on Egil's metal glove.

"Sink into the abysses of fire!" announced Gennaro, sticking his crosier once again into the asphalt.

A hole opened, advancing toward them. Taro stretched his arm out, protected by the glove, and from his open palm a mighty shield of white light appeared, blocking the course of the hole.

"Behold the light, Gennaro," Taro said, as flocks of doves soared behind him. He almost did not recognize his own voice. "Do not persist in error; join us!"

He closed his gloved hand, and immediately the hole filled with lava and closed again. Soon after, the fiery pool began to bubble. With a tremendous roar, a column of lava in the shape of a dragon's head rose skyward, only to immediately plunge with open jaws toward Gennaro. The Saint was enveloped by the flow. The Martyrs, protected by the glowing shield, saw a knight in armor draw his spear from those smoking remains.

"Egil!" shouted Taro. He immediately hugged his friend, moved. "I knew you would make it! Are you okay?"

"If you hadn't made me take off my glove, I would be better, but…everything is okay!" replied Egil showing his arm with the missing hand.

"No matter how many times you knock me down," announced a familiar voice behind them, "I will always get up. With God's help I will defeat you!"

The four Martyrs turned around: Gennaro was up again, in one piece. The ground shook again, and from Mount Vesuvius came ominous rumblings. The Saint hurled his crosier; in mid-air, it transformed into spears: one for each of them. Taro closed his eyes and, impelled by a sudden inspiration, walked with open arms toward the incoming threat. As if they had struck an invisible wall, the spears abruptly halted their course in the air. Incredulous, Gennaro saw them fall to the ground where they fused together. Promptly, Egil picked up the crosier and threw it into Gennaro, spearing the Saint with his own weapon.

"This is impossible," he mumbled as the crosier pierced his chest. When he fell to the ground, a pool of lava appeared under him. He began to sink, and soon his body was dissolved. Only the golden tiara with the Latin cross was left.

Egil knelt beside the steaming pool and prayed. At that moment, his wounded arm glowed with a crimson light. After he finished his prayer, the man made the sign of the cross. The purple aura faded, revealing two healthy hands.

"Amen," he concluded in a whisper.

XVIII

The Most Holy Capital of God's Kingdom on Earth, the Sistine Chapel

Saint Thomas enters the Sistine Chapel!"

As the delicately engraved doors slowly turned on their big hinges, the Saint scurried into the large, frescoed room. In his haste, he almost tripped on his long robe.

"Your Most Excellent Holiness, we have received very important information," he announced, panting.

"Please, Chrismatics," said the young patriarch, "leave us alone."

"Fiat voluntas tua," replied together the guardians.

One by one, they left the room in a silence broken only by distant echoes of sacred hymns.

Peter II Romano's eyes seemed veiled by sadness.

"Thomas, I hope that the news you bring is good."

"Some pieces are, Your Most Excellent Holiness. And others aren't, I am afraid."

"Let's begin with the good news," suggested the patriarch,

massaging his temples. "In this difficult time, we really need good news."

"We know where the Holy Grail is."

"Excellent! Praise the Lord! Have you recovered it?"

"Not yet, Your Most Excellent Holiness," explained the Saint. "But it will be done in the next few hours. We know it is in Castel del Monte, a magnificent walled building in the province of…"

"I know where it is," the young patriarch interrupted him. "Tell me, what proof do we have that the Holy Grail is really in that fortress?"

"Unfortunately, this is one of the pieces of bad news," replied the Saint, lowering his eyes. "The place where the Grail is held was indicated in an ancient manuscript, kept in secret by Monsignor Centritto of Naples, who had met recently the Anti-Christ and his heralds…"

"I knew it!"

The patriarch's eyes glared with anger. Thomas felt ashamed of himself.

"I knew those heretics were still hiding among our sheep. And I still smell their horrible stench!" the young patriarch continued.

Six flaming wings sprouted from his back, emanating an intense light.

"Anti-Christ, damn you!" he shouted in a terrible voice, taking flight. "There isn't a place for you in the Kingdom of God! You will end up in Hell amid atrocious suffering!"

The Saint, blinded by the divine glow, prostrated himself until his forehead touched the floor. An intense warmth lapped at his body, as if he were in a burning house. That superhuman voice rumbled in his ears like a thunder, but he could not grasp the words' meaning.

After a moment, everything went silent. Shyly, the Saint lifted his head and saw Peter II Romano lying motionless on the ground before his throne.

"Your Most Excellent Holiness!" he said, agitated, rushing in his aid. "Oh mercy! Answer me! Your Most Excellent Holiness!"

The patriarch gave no signs of life. In disbelief, the Saint lifted the patriarch's head.

"Your Holiness, please, answer me."

A warm tear ran down his cheek.

The patriarch gasped, his eyes flickering open.

"Your Most Excellent Holiness! Are you all right? For a moment I feared…"

"I am fine," replied Peter II Romano, getting up as though he hadn't been unconscious a moment before. Thomas noticed that the patriarch's eyes had very dark circles under them, and that his expression betrayed pain.

"You should rest," suggested Thomas in a fatherly way. "You haven't fully recovered from the bloody battles you had against the Luciferals."

"I can't stay idle while my people suffer," the patriarch replied vehemently. "I must eradicate all the evil in this world as soon as possible. And now, go on with your report…"

"As I was saying, two fragments of the Gospel venerated by the

Hand of God have been found, one in Naples and the other one in Cascia, amidst the remains of the fire. They are both on their way and should get here soon."

"Good. You must tell Augustine to leave Cascia and go to Castel del Monte as soon as possible. I want that place to become an impregnable fortress."

"Fiat voluntas tua."

"And what do we know about Anthony and Rita?"

"We don't know anything yet about Anthony, unfortunately. As for Rita, her relics have been found recently among the ruins, perfectly kept despite the terrible explosion."

"The loss of Rita saddens all the people of the Church Dei Invicti Operae," said the patriarch, his voice broken by emotion. "Make arrangements for her holy relics to be transferred to Sancta Sanctorum. Let's do everything we can to make another transubstantiation happen. I want her back with us."

"Speaking of this, I have excellent news," replied Thomas. "His Almighty has granted transubstantiation to the seventeenth holy relic."

The patriarch's eyes sparkled.

"Thank you, Lord!" the patriarch exclaimed, rising to his feet as he turned his eyes and palms upward in prayer. "This sign of your benevolence means that our triumph is near."

"Longinus, reborn from the relic, has shown an unwavering faith and unparalleled devotion to the cause," added the Saint smiling.

"Send him to Castel del Monte as well," ordered Peter II Romano, sitting back down on his throne. "I want to be sure that the Grail is recovered and that the Anti-Christ and his heralds are defeated."

"Fiat voluntas tua," said Thomas, kneeling before the leader of his faith.

XIX

Contrada Finizio (Andria)

A lone car traveled a narrow road between olive groves and farm fields. In the distance, an imposing castle, sparkling silver thanks to the moonlight, overlooked the valley atop a hill. In the car, there was only silence. Egil, who was driving, had his eyes fixed on the road. Next to him, Ciccio slept soundly.

Taro admired the night landscape. He had spent so many holidays in those places! His eyes fell on the outline of the castle on the hill, but his mind lost itself in the chirping of the cicadas during a summer afternoon. He was eight and his uncle Alex had taken him on a trip to see the castle, with Pia.

"Sabino, my little one, why don't you want to enter with us?" Pia, who had already developed an inordinate amount of patience, had asked him.

And Sabino, whimpering with his fists over his eyes, had replied: "Let's leave! That castle belongs to the Black Knight."

He smiled thinking about his childhood obsession. Still, he did not budge and made his uncle Alex and Pia play ladies and knights outside the castle. He never went back after that day.

He turned toward Arian. She was silent with her head against the window. Her eyes were always hidden behind her sunglasses, but Sabino thought she was sleeping. Even someone as strong as Arian could get tired.

What a woman… he thought.

Her leather clothes sparkled under the moonlight, making her look like a mermaid. Her breasts moved following the rhythm of her breathing like a sensual dance. Taro felt a powerful heat invading his body, and he moved closer to her as his heart began to race. He was torn: follow his crazy desire or stay faithful to Sharon?

In the chaotic whirlwind of emotions inside him, an idea surfaced. Determined, he reached for Arian's glasses. He wanted to take them off and finally look at her without barriers. If he met her eyes, perhaps his doubts would dissipate. He would turn away from her or he would get sucked into a whirlwind of passion.

Arian sighed in such a light and sweet way that the boy, for a moment, stopped. But then his fingers brushed the dark lenses reflecting the moon. Another moment and the last veil would fall…

"I wouldn't do it."

He withdrew his hand immediately and turned around.

"Come close," ordered Ciccio.

Ashamed, Taro leaned toward the passenger seat.

"It isn't what you think," he mumbled, his face red.

"Don't say minchiate. We're not stupid. Everyone can see you are attracted to her."

"I wanted…" Taro sighed. "I just wanted to look her in the eyes."

"Really? Just that?"

A thousand words flooded Taro's mind.

"Anyway, I don't care what you feel for her," said Ciccio. "I just wanted to warn you not to take her glasses off."

"Why?"

As if in cahoots, Ciccio gestured him to come even closer. Taro brought his ear as close as possible to Ciccio's mouth who said whispering: "Do you remember Sharon?"

A sense of piercing guilt gripped Taro, who remembered the first, tender kiss he exchanged with his girlfriend from London.

"Arian's colleague," Ciccio clarified, drawing Taro from his memories.

"Yes, I remember. But what does she have to do with this? We were talking about…"

"She has everything to do with this. Do you remember that one day Arian followed her into the Archives' basement?"

"Yes, and so?"

As much as it was possible, Ciccio lowered his voice even more. "What I am about to tell you must stay a secret, lo capisti?"

"A secret?"

"Will you give me your word of honor, yes or no?"

"Okay…calm down. You have my word. I won't say anything to anyone."

"To make the story short, Sharon was in cahoots with the Luciferals…"

"Fuck!"

"In the Archives, Arian discovered Sharon and others that were celebrating a black mass in order to summon some Luciferals."

"But…in the Archives? Among holy relics?"

"'Where there is much light, the shadow is blackest,' Goethe used to say."

Taro was surprised by that unexpected quote—he would never have thought that Ciccio was interested in literature—and kept quiet, letting his friend continue.

"Arian was captured and tortured atrociously. And Sharon, with her own very hands, gouged out Arian's eyes as punishment for having seen something she should never had."

The boy, horrified, wanted to say something.

But he couldn't.

"It was then that the consubstantiation with the holy relics of Saint Lucy happened. Arian barely made it, and no one heard again from Sharon and the others."

"Poor Arian…"

"This is our secret. None of us has ever seen Arian without her sunglasses. I don't believe it would be a pleasant sight."

"Thank you," Taro said. "That explains a lot, and I am sorry if…"

"Never mind, Taro!" interjected Egil. "Arian will tell you about it, sooner or later, but until then…"

"Not a single word!" concluded Ciccio, briefly holding a single finger up to his lips.

The car slowed abruptly. In front of them there was a thick fog bank.

"Shit!" Egil shouted, driving carefully. "Where is it coming from?"

Taro rested his forehead against the window: a milky fog hid the view in every direction.

"Damn! The fog lights of this shitty car don't work."

"Hey, watch your mouth," replied Ciccio, offended. "Next time, I really want to see what kind of car *you* can get."

"Stop it," Egil growled. "Look out and tell me if the road is straight or if there are bends."

Egil shifted into first gear as Ciccio leaned out the window.

"That's it, Egil, keep on going straight ahead!"

As soon as Ciccio finished talking, the left side of the car shuddered and sank, producing a metallic clunk. The engine stopped suddenly.

"Everything all right, guys?" asked Arian, who had been jolted awaken by all the commotion.

"I don't think so," replied Taro, getting out of the car with Egil and Ciccio.

He noticed that the front left wheel was off the road, in a small rocky ditch. Egil, handling a pocket flashlight, bent down to assess the situation.

"Fuck you, Ciccio!" he swore as the beam of light danced on the gears. "The axle shaft broke. Where the hell were you looking?"

"I was looking at la bella faccia tua," replied Ciccio, gesturing to Egil's "pretty" face as he lit up a cigarette. "You can't see a minchia thing with this fog! Should I call the tow truck?"

"Knock it off, you two!" Arian scolded. "Honestly, I can't even take a short nap..."

"What do we do now?" asked Taro.

"We walk, what else?" suggested Arian. "After all, the fog isn't only a disadvantage. It will help us not being seen."

"And my car?" asked a worried Ciccio. "We can't leave it here all alone, can we?"

"C'mon!" Egil said, rolling his eyes. "You know it isn't your car."

"Follow me. I'll lead the way," said Arian, walking with confidence into the fog. "Watch where you step."

Marveling at her incredible sensory skills, Taro followed her with Egil and Ciccio, stepping into the whitish mist. As the four walked on, the cold's grip tightened around their bodies and their hearts. Like an evanescent ghost, the fog crept into their clothes, and their breath condensed into steam as their footsteps crumbled the frost in the fields.

"Hey, do you hear them? The voices?" whispered Egil.

They stopped. The fog was everywhere, like the infinite ocean surrounding a castaway. The cold wind carried with it echoes of distant songs.

"I don't like this one bit," Egil said. "Be ready!"

Arian, following an inexplicable instinct, began to run. Howling, a big gray wolf with a golden bracelet on one paw kept up with her. Egil and Taro, left behind, followed the elusive silhouette of Arian and Ciccio into the thick blankets of fog, doing their best to avoid skeletal trees, thorny bushes, and roots. Gradually, the songs became clearer, until the Martyrs ended up in a glade. Festive hymns rose from a crowd of people. They were dancing around a big fire, too busy to notice the Martyrs. Next to the fire, there was a walnut tree, a hundred feet tall, extending its branches over much of the clearing.

Under the tree, a wooden throne bore a man wearing a goat mask with three horns. In front of him, a long queue of deformed people paid him homage.

"Hey, where are we? Is this a Halloween party?" asked Taro, panting after the run.

"No, it is a Concionem, a cursed gathering presided over by a Luciferal. I've met him," explained Arian, out of breath.

She took her guns out and fired, blasting away two of the goat's horns. The songs stopped, and the clearing filled with cries of panic and total chaos.

As his severed horns grew back with shocking speed, the Luciferal got up. He had fiery eyes, black and curly hair, and a long and shaggy beard. Under his human-looking torso, a donkey tail wagged behind chicken's legs ending in webbed feet.

With a terrifying roar, he incited those present. "My children, here is your banquet! Satiate yourselves with these unholy individuals!"

Many fled, but some others made their way forward toward the Martyrs. Their faces were distorted by unnatural grimaces, their eyes white and their limbs asymmetrical and muscular.

"I have finally found you, Leonardo. I will make you pay for all your horrendous crimes!" shouted Arian, running toward the goat.

Taro, terrified, saw the Luciferal burst into a loud laugh, turning his back and lifting his donkey tail. A demonic face, placed at the buttocks' level, began spewing insults and profanity.

Arian fired at him, but the face repelled all the bullets by simply blowing them away. A deformed and sinewy man stood in front of Taro, but Egil, who was already wearing his silvery armor, immediately hit the cultist with his spear. Ciccio, now a wolf, lunged at the throat of another deformed creature, and Arian sneaked under the walnut tree, following the goat-like demon. Egil and Taro did the same.

"You won't escape me," threatened Arian, firing repeatedly. "The party is over, this time forever!"

"Wretched mortal female," thundered the Luciferal, deftly dodging each bullet. "I am the Concionem's Grand Master. I decide when the gathering is over, and I still want to have a lot of fun."

With superhuman agility, he climbed the walnut tree higher and higher. When he reached its top, he bent down, and under the donkey tail, his second face appeared again, speaking in a cavernous voice.

"Hear me, Juglans, mother of this gathering! Show our enemies your true self! Listen to the Grand Master's voice and allow your countless children to satiate their cravings on these perverse blasphemous people!"

Arian jumped back just in time to avoid a huge wooden hand that launched itself out from the tree trunk. As she somersaulted in the air, she fired repeatedly in the direction of the Luciferal. The tree branches moved with incredible speed and deflected each bullet. Buds sprouted from the branches, turning immediately into humungous walnuts that fell to the ground. Each walnut shuddered as it hit the earth, and deformed beings emerged from the shells to walk menacingly toward the Martyrs.

Ciccio, still a gray wolf, stood in front of Taro to protect him. The horde of wretched beings edged closer and closer. Some tripped on their lopsided legs, others dragged themselves forward on three legs, while others still galloped on five legs as more walnuts fell from the branches.

"Shit!" cursed Egil, piercing their enemies with his spear. "How many are there?"

Arian replaced the magazines and fired again. The power of her bullets was devastating. Every monstrous being hit caught fire, quickly turning into a pile of ashes. But no matter how many she destroyed, more came.

The Luciferal snickered in a terrifying voice: "I don't know who you are, but you and your friends are going to die horribly. The prolific mother Juglans is inexhaustible. Your bullets, on the other hand, are about to end."

The clearing swarmed with demonic beings who, like waves of a stormy sea, crashed against the Martyrs' defenses, which grew weaker and weaker. When everything seemed lost, Taro heard the Concionem's Grand Master howling in pain. The entire walnut tree was on fire, and it began to writhe and scream like a human being.

Altogether, the children of Juglans did the same, as if they were also on fire. One by one, all the tree branches dissolved into black dust. In the same way, the beings crumbled. In the end, only the tree trunk was left to slowly burn.

The Luciferal did not even have the time to lift his muddy face before his forehead was met with two guns.

"Where is Sharon, you bastard?" Arian urged him.

Taro, next to her, looked at the shrub again. A white light caught the attention of everyone except the resolute Arian: among the flames blazing from the remains of the trunk appeared a figure, who was now walking toward them. The man wore a gray monk's habit with a hood lowered over his head to hide the face, and in his arms, he held a beautiful smiling child.

"Speak! Where is Sharon?" repeated Arian, thrusting her guns at the Luciferal. But before the creature could speak, his form dissolved into a pentacle of gray ashes.

"He won't escape, não preocupe," announced the monk.

"Minchia, Anthony!" said Ciccio, lighting a cigarette. "We thought we were done for! We owe you a favor."

"Can I ask you then," said the Saint, "not to smoke in front of the child?"

Ciccio coughed, embarrassed, immediately tossing the cigarette on the ground and putting it out with his shoe. The child squirmed, and Anthony had to put him down.

Egil held out his hand and thanked him.

"Não...don't thank me. It is all the child's doing. It is he who guided me here."

Everyone turned to look at the child, who had run to hug Taro.

"Tell me, vejo, I see clearly in you the pure espírito of the Saints, but you aren't Saints..."

"Believe me, we also don't know our nature with certainty," replied Arian, reloading her weapons.

"There is one thing, though, we have no doubts about," added Taro, who was now holding the child in his arms. "We are ready to sacrifice anything in order to save humankind."

The child smacked a kiss onto Taro's cheek and then, once again on the ground, crawled toward Anthony.

"I feel the same as you do and that is why I had predicted a perigoso—a dangerous gathering of Luciferals here."

The facial expression of the child became suddenly sad. He stretched his arm and pointed his little finger right in front of him.

"Now," Anthony continued, "temos que partir..." At Taro's blank look, Anthony translated, "I am afraid I have to go... There are other rituals just like this one that are taking place and I must stop them."

"See you," Egil said. "We are going to the castle. Good luck!"

The Saint put his hood back up and walked into the mist.

"Go your way and boa sorte to you too," replied Anthony, disappearing into the vast expanse of white.

"Leonardo, that bastard!" hissed Arian.

"How do you know that Luciferal?" Taro asked her, concerned about her reply.

"I have a score to settle with him... With him and Sharon."

Castel del Monte (Andria)

The slope of the terrain gradually climbed, and the roughness of the area made it difficult to keep up with Arian. Unclear noises mixed with Taro's labored breathing, as they both raced toward the castle that only Arian could see.

The noises slowly became clearer: groans, gunfire and then a haunting hissing sound.

A panting figure ran toward them. It was a policeman, pale with shock.

"There are too many of them," he said, automaton-like, as more gunshots were heard in the distance. "Hundreds and hundreds of damned Luciferals. And the Chrismatics are too few…where is the help? I don't want to die!"

Taro approached him, realizing that the man had a bad wound on his left leg.

"Easy, brother," he murmured, resting a hand on the officer's increasingly nervous quadriceps. "Have faith…"

His bandana lit up and a white light illuminated the wound.

"It doesn't hurt anymore!" The officer said in disbelief. "You must be—"

"Yes, we are the help," Egil interrupted, letting the officer draw his own conclusion. "But now, run and call for more, okay?"

"Yes, sir! I will go immediately!"

Taro found himself smiling as the policeman vanished into the darkness.

"Let's go see what kind of beasts we are dealing with," Ciccio said to them.

The Martyrs went deeper into the fog, in the direction of the gunfire and wailing, which grew louder and louder, closer and closer. Soon, they found themselves outside the woods, at the foot of a tall hill. On its top stood the octagonal shape of Castel del Monte, like a crown on the head of a king.

In front of its entrance, a scattered group of Chrismatics fought against a multitude of snake-men who, amid hisses and gurgles, pressed to enter. Along the narrow path leading to the top, humanoid-faced cobras advanced toward the gate. At the base of the hill, dozens of police cars were overturned and on fire.

A sea of corpses was strewn on the ground.

"All these people couldn't have come here by accident. Even the Luciferals!" observed Taro, shocked.

"The patriarch knows everything, it's obvious," retorted Arian. "At this point, it makes no difference anymore. Are you all ready?"

"Let's rock and roll!" Egil said, a dangerous light in his eyes.

Ciccio turned into a big mongoose wagging its tail, eager to fight. Taro was enveloped in a ball of light. He made the sign of the cross and energetically incited his comrades: "Follow me, my friends!"

Running furiously up the path, he swept over numerous cobras, which were knocked away from his protective aura like pins hit by a bowling ball. Meanwhile, the mongoose threw himself on other beasts, sinking his teeth behind their heads. Each snake tried to shake its head furiously, but the mongoose would not let go until his prey fell lifeless to the ground.

On the other side, Arian fired her alchemical bullets, avoiding the cobras' bites. As soon as the reptiles were hit, they began to blow out of proportion until they exploded loudly amid a cascade of green, venomous blood. Thanks to her, Egil and Taro reached the main entrance, now protected only by two surviving Chrismatics.

"Showtime!" shouted Egil, impaling two cobras. "Watch my back and everything will be okay!"

"Of course, bro!" Taro promised. "They won't get past."

Dozens of sharp fangs shattered on the white sphere protecting them as Taro's friend skewered rows of slimy snake-men, spattering their blood everywhere.

The fight lasted a long time until Egil nailed to the ground the last head of the last remaining living monster, driving his spearhead out of its mouth. An unnatural silence fell on the valley, still enveloped in the fog as far as the eye could see. In the woods, here and there, one could see the orange glow of a few large fires. Egil removed his helmet and ran a hand through his salt and pepper hair.

"Is it over?" stammered Taro, falling to his knees.

He felt exhausted, but at the same time his body was quivering with adrenaline. He looked up and saw that Arian and Ciccio had reached them unharmed.

"Picciò, everything okay?" Ciccio asked him.

"My legs are a bit shaky…but other than that, yeah. I'm okay."

As he walked through the snake corpses, he was overwhelmed by memories and special moments of his childhood. He turned around quickly.

"The Black Knight," he thought shaking his head. "What nonsense."

When he tried to take a step, though, he realized he wasn't able to move.

"Hey, what's happening?" he cursed.

"What the minchia…" cursed Ciccio, also immobilized.

A violent earthquake shook the ground, and the Martyrs could do nothing but fall.

"Fools!" thundered a tone-deaf voice. "I adore seeing you suffer." A being with three long horns on its head walked up the path toward them.

"Leonardo, you bastard!" shouted Arian, trying to force her immobilized fingers to squeeze the triggers of her guns. She succeeded just enough to fire—two bullets reached the Luciferal, but they bounced off him like tennis balls on the court. The being raised its clawed hands toward the sky, and immediately, a circle of flames surrounded the valley, separating it from the forest.

A green aura enveloped Ciccio, who in an instant turned into an eagle. But the majestic bird wasn't able to spread his wings and turned into a rhino instead. Still, he couldn't get up. The overwhelming force beating down on them was too strong.

Taro felt the weight of a hundred buildings on him and his energies were slowly sapped away. Getting more frightened by the moment, he saw the creature kneel, raising its arms to the sky.

"I offer you these victims, o great Volac! Hear the painful, vengeful cry of your children and answer our call!"

The corpses of the snake-men shook with violent convulsions and rose, puppets moved by invisible strings. Some began to slither up the path while others gathered around the Concionem's Grand Master.

"Great Volac, in exchange for the life of these murderers, I ask you to retrieve for me the Holy Grail!"

He rested his goat muzzle on the trembling ground. A strong current arose, shaking the flames around.

Taro thought he was about to die.

A deafening roar swept over the entire valley. But instead of certain doom, gigantic waves of crystal-clear water advanced toward both sides of the hill, sweeping everything away and putting out the fire.

"No!" cried Leonardo, stunned.

Its fury exhausted, the water drained away. The last flickering flame was extinguished by the wind. Only a long strip on ash remained of the fire circle.

"Vile foul goat," said an unknown voice, "get ready to receive just punishment for your misdeeds!"

Taro turned and saw a bearded man, wearing a tunic and a fur around his shoulders, walking up the path toward them, shrouded in a golden aura. His face wore a proud expression, and in his right hand, he held a staff ending in a cross.

"John!" the creature blurted out. "It is impossible. You were in prison..."

"There are no obstacles that can stop the justice of the Almighty."'

"Justice?" repeated the Luciferal, chuckling. "Don't lecture me! You, better than anyone else, can understand how it feels to be in the shoes of the outlaws. After all your sacrifices and absolute devotion to the cause, this is the reward they are offering you: prison!"

The Saint paused, closing his eyes, as the strong wind rippled the water surrounding the hill. "Lamb of God," he said, "protect your apostles!"

A great sphere of light descended from the sky and floated toward the earth, gradually becoming more and more evanescent; it rested in front of the castle's entrance and gently encompassed the four Martyrs.

"Listen to me, John, you and I are the same: two outlaws. Why not co-operate?" Leonardo proposed.

The Saint snapped his eyes open, causing the Luciferal to fall silent. "Joining you would be unthinkable," John said firmly. "His Most Excellent Holiness has inflicted punishment upon me, yet the Almighty's will has absolved me! And it is precisely the justice of the Almighty that will punish you now!"

"Calm down and think," Leonardo countered. "If the Almighty

has justly acquitted you, it means that His Most Excellent Holiness condemned you unjustly."

The goat was backing away cautiously while John strode toward him.

"This is what happens to those who believe they possess the Truth: you do wrong," the Luciferal continued. "There is not a single human that knows it!"

An unexpected boulder made the Luciferal trip and fall clumsily to the ground. John loomed over him from above, pointing the crucifix at his forehead.

"For once you said something sensible," he admitted, "because no human being is allowed to know the Truth."

The beast smiled, showing his rotten teeth. "We completely agree then! If you remain with the Church, you will contribute to creating a future where someone will tell you what is the right thing to do. Join us, instead! With the power of the Holy Grail, together we'll create a world where everyone is free."

But John just chuckled. "I am neither with the Church nor am I against it," he confessed. "The Almighty guides my steps and enlightens my judgment. I only do His will!"

The Luciferal felt the cold metal of the crucifix touch its forehead and tried to run away, but an invincible power prevented it from doing so.

"Beast! I, John, son of Zechariah, condemn you in the name of the God of Adam, Noah, and Abraham. Divine light, purify this wretched being and purge Creation of its troublesome presence!"

The Saint grabbed his staff with both hands, raising it high in front of him. The crucifix emitted a cone of light that struck the goat head, which let out a shrill scream. Its flesh melted as black smoke wafted from its eyes and mouth. Only a big goat skull with three horns remained.

"Amen."

John was about to make the sign of the cross when a strong earthquake shook the hill. Taro and the other Martyrs were still paralyzed, so the Saint lifted the staff toward them, staring at each one intensely. In a moment, the Martyrs regained control of their bodies and stumbled to their feet.

"Get into the castle!" he ordered them.

Ciccio turned toward the building; rubble and stones were crumbling from the upper floors.

"Are you sure? Minchia, everything is collapsing here!"

"C'mon, let's do as he says," Egil urged. "We must have faith!"

"What the minchia are you saying? Have you ever read earthquake regulations? Getting out of enclosed places is the first rule."

"Get into the castle, hurry!" John called as the tremors became stronger.

Egil grabbed Ciccio by the sleeve of his jacket and pulled him toward the main door, followed by the others. Taro had just enough time to see the Saint lift his staff toward the leaden sky. For a moment, he thought he saw a two-headed dragon among the clouds, but his view was soon enveloped by the darkness of the castle. In front of him stood a broad figure covered in a red cloak. Between his hands, there was a crosier.

Out of the frying pan… Taro thought.

"Welcome! My name is Nicholas. I am the protector of the city of Bari and defender of this castle at the request of His Most Excellent Holiness. And now let's see what you are made of..."

He struck his crosier on the ground four times; one by one all the Martyrs fell down unconscious.

XXI

A Dream

The hallway was dark, but Arian had no difficulty finding her way around.

She knew this maze all too well, and nothing would stop her this time. She reached the elevator and pushed the call button; the doors opened with a buzz. Looking behind her shoulder, she walked in quickly and inserted a small key in the hole just below the button panel. She turned it and the doors closed. The elevator started its descent, slowly. Crouching against the wall, the woman drew her guns. She smiled, thinking about the expression her prey would make.

The elevator stopped and the doors opened. Lost in her thoughts, a blond girl in her thirties walked in, holding a few volumes in her hands. She immediately found herself staring at two guns pointed at her temples: the books fell on the ground, causing a muffled rustle in the small space.

"It has been so long, Sharon!" Arian's voice was harsh, firm.

"Oh my God!" Sharon exclaimed.

"Surprised to see me?" Arian placed one of her guns under Sharon's chin. "Did you think I was dead? Of course, if it were up to you..."

"It is not what you think," Sharon stammered, shaking.

"Oh really? Then who organized the black mass down here? Who lured me there, deceiving me?"

Faced with accusations, Sharon began to sob, cowering in a corner.

"You are the one who scarred me," continued Arian. "You are the one who ruined my life… And now you'll pay!"

"No, please! It wasn't my fault! I did not want to, I swear! I wasn't in control of myself!"

"Why?" Arian insisted, getting one of her guns ready to fire. "Why did you do it? You were my best friend."

"Listen to me, please…" whimpered Sharon. "There was a demon inside me. It was him, Leonardo, who made me commit those crimes! I don't even remember them…"

"Damn goat…"

"I was drinking tea and I had the photocopies of the papyrus in front of me. There were only a few days left before the deadline, and I had not been able to translate a single line…"

Arian pressed a button on the control panel, and the elevator doors closed again. They rose as Arian looked down at the other woman.

"Why didn't you let me help you?" she asked Sharon, disappointed. "We would have made it together, as always."

"You don't know how frustrating it is to see your problems solved by others," Sharon moaned bitterly. "You always had the solution. I wanted to prove to myself that I, too, was able to help you… That was when I met Leonardo. He sat next to me: he was charming, refined, and vastly educated. He offered me his total availability to translate the papyrus. In return he asked for only my signature…"

"Your signature?" Arian gasped. "Did you realize what you had done?"

"I do now," she replied, bursting into tears. "You know, I never believed in the soul and the devil and all those things… I thought it was such a great bargain…"

"A great bargain?" Arian lost her temper and slapped her former friend. "You sold your soul to that scumbag! You betrayed our friendship! You allowed him to ruin your life *and* mine!"

"I am sorry," Sharon pleaded. "I just wanted to help you. I don't even remember everything I did while I was at the mercy of that demon. If the exorcist at my church hadn't set me free, who knows what else I would have done…"

"Leonardo is no longer inside you, is he?" Arian pointed her guns at the other woman's forehead. "Too bad. I would have killed two birds with one stone."

"No, please!" pleaded Sharon. "I didn't want to!"

"That's enough! Goodbye."

The elevator doors opened with the usual buzzing sound. Sharon closed her eyes and heard two deafening gunshots.

Panting, the woman opened her eyes again. Her scream rose very high as she caught sight, in the dark hallway, of a horrible creature lying on the floor with two holes in its chest.

Of Arian, not a trace.

"Next!"

At the announcement of the beautiful hostess in black suit, the first in line entered the Virgo Studios building. Behind him, Sabino was trying to warm himself as best as he could under the snowflakes of that harsh winter evening.

Just a bit longer and he would enter. The moment was almost here. Behind him, there was only one more man in line.

"I can't wait! I am so pumped!" Sabino said turning to him.

"That's normal. It's your first audition," said Gabry with a shrug.

Sabino's friend was almost as tall as a model, with dark hair and eyes, and he wore a tailored dark leather jacket. His face had barely hardened, unmarked by life, and he looked thirty at most. In short, a real badass. "I was all electrified my first time too," he added.

"I'm also freezing to death," Sabino joked, rubbing his hands together. "We've been waiting out here for more than six hours."

"Six hours is nothing! One time I waited outside for twelve! Today is my last chance, and I won't budge until they hear me."

"Your last chance?" Sabino repeated. "What do you mean?"

"Well, I've been trying to break through for ten years. My parents gave me an ultimatum: I either sign a contract this week or they cut me off. And at that point I will have to go back to the village to work in my dad's store..."

"What?" said Sabino worried. "You are telling me this only now? We have to rap together! You made me passionate about rap! You can't give up just like this."

"You know how it is, S.P., I am not that young anymore," concluded Gabry, looking down.

Sabino became sad: such talk depressed him, and he didn't even want to think that sooner or later, he too might face the same problem.

"Hey, don't be like that!" exclaimed Gabry, giving him a vigorous pat on the back. "This is our fucking chance, and we are going to take it!"

"You speak the fucking truth, bro! Let's show those guys who we are!"

At that exact moment, the door opened, and the attractive hostess reappeared: her platinum blond hair, her crimson lipstick, and her delicate mole made Sabino think of Marilyn Monroe, but wearing an impeccable blue suit bearing the Virgo Studios logo.

"I apologize, sirs," she began with a fake polite smile. "We thank you for waiting but the organizers are sorry to inform you that they only have time to judge one final candidate. Which one of you is next?"

The news left the two surprised as they looked at each other.

"He is next!" said Sabino impulsively, pointing at Gabry.

The older man winced. "Me?"

"Please, this way," the hostess urged him. "We have to wrap up soon."

"Thank you, bro! I owe you one." Gabry hugged his friend and walked toward the entrance.

"Go and show them!" Sabino cheered him on, moved by their friendship.

Gabry ran inside the big building and the glass door closed behind him.

Sabino turned and walked slowly under the snow, when suddenly he saw a familiar figure.

It was Uncle Alex.

"Sabino!" the man called him, surprised. "I have finally found you! I went to pick you up at school, but you weren't there..."

"Uncle, it is so nice to see you! I was about to..."

"What are you doing here?" asked the bishop, tapping his left foot nervously. "And why did you play hooky?"

"You know...they told me that today around here a missionary was going to speak about his experiences in Africa and I came to listen to him..."

"A missionary, sure!" replied his uncle with a stern look. "And was his name by any chance Don Virgo Studios?"

Sabino held up his hands. "Wait, it isn't what you think..."

"How many times do I have to tell you that lying is a sin?" The bishop grabbed him by the ear. "Tonight, no dinner until you say at least twenty Hail Mary first!"

"No, please," begged Sabino through clenched teeth in a grimace of pain. "Not the Hail Mary!"

"Yes, you are!" continued Alessandro, tugging at him. "And at home we will talk about your bad habit of skipping school!"

They both disappeared, swallowed by the snow.

"Lynx reporting, over!"

Egil brought the transceiver to his mouth and said, "Lion on, listening. Tell me everything, Lynx!"

"No movement to report."

"Very well, Lynx! Carefully drive out the Boar. We will arrive in time for the roast."

"Roger that. Over and out!"

Egil handed the device to one of the other three passengers of the jeep, which was jolting over the desert dunes. They were all wearing heavy camouflages and wielding assault rifles. No one made a sound. A few palms could be seen on the horizon amid the wind-blown sand.

The jeep stopped a few hundred feet from the trees. Egil got out first and with a wave of his hand prompted the others to do the same. They approached cautiously, slowly climbing the last dune separating them from their target.

Reaching the top, Egil leaned over and saw a small oasis dotted with tents. Three men, wearing the same camouflage as Egil and his team, were standing near a small lake. One of them noticed Egil and began waving his arms.

“Let’s go! Let’s go!” Egil ordered.

The seven soldiers gathered under the palm trees, sheltered by the scorching sun. Around them, there were bodies of men, women, children, and animals, all horribly slaughtered.

“Lynx reporting for duty, sir!” one of the soldiers at attention said.

“At ease, Lynx!” Egil said, looking at the gruesome view. “What the hell happened here?”

“We got here about fifteen minutes ago, sir, and we found this. There are no survivors in the entire oasis.”

“If I may say, sir,” another soldier intervened, bent over a child’s corpse, “they were all killed by gunshot wounds. And it looks like they’ve been dead for at least a day…”

“Thank you, Hyena. Did you find any of the terrorists among them?”

“No, sir.”

Egil turned away, kicking the ground. “Bastards! They chose this oasis as their base, but the population must have found the courage to rebel…”

The soldiers stood there, in silence, as the hot desert wind lifted clouds of sand.

“C’mon boys!” Egil said finally. “Let’s scour the oasis! We need to figure out where those sons of bitches have gone! I swear we will capture them!”

“Yes sir!” the soldiers replied in unison.

After a few minutes, Egil was summoned into one of the tents.

"Here, sir," a soldier said, handing him a plate. Egil looked at it. It was dirty with food remains and blood.

"See here, sir? It looks like writing in Arabic to me. I don't know the language, but considering that old man over there was holding it tight to his chest…"

"Excellent work, Hound! Call Owl immediately."

In a blink of an eye, a female soldier entered the tent, standing right away at attention.

"Owl reporting, sir!"

"At ease, at ease… In your opinion, tell me, is this writing?"

He showed her the plate.

"Oh my!" she replied, surprised. "It's Arabic. It says…Lod, sir."

"Lod?" Egil frowned. "What does it mean?"

"It is the name of a village. It is quite far from here though. I don't know if it can also mean something else… I would need to look it up in a dictionary."

"Well," Egil concluded, approaching the old man's body, "maybe this is the last message this man wanted to entrust us with."

With a gentle stroke, he closed the old man's eyes.

"C'mon, boys! We have a clue to follow. I want everyone here in two minutes."

"I'll run to tell the others, sir!" said Hound.

"Shall I get the jeep ready, sir?" asked Owl.

"No," Egil replied, staring at her, "we still have an important mission to accomplish here. These courageous people need a proper burial."

The female soldier nodded and left the tent. Alone, Egil looked again at the old man. His face, marked by time, which had initially been twisted in a grimace of pain, seemed relaxed.

In the dark room, a few timid rays of sunlight filtered through the uneven boards, barely illuminating a man tied to a chair. His head was reclined to his chest, his shirt greasy and blood-stained.

The air was heavy with the strong smell of dung. The only sounds were the rooting of pigs and the clucking of chickens. Four dark-clothed men staked out the four corners of the room.

Suddenly, a door burst open. Dazzled by the light, the man tied to the chair lifted his head and saw a tall and massive figure enter the room slowly.

"Santuzzo, is it really you?" asked the newcomer. "My heart aches to see you like this..."

"Don Ciccio, please..." begged Santuzzo, looking tired. "Help me!"

"I really wish I could, but your position is indefensible, lo capisti?"

"You know better than me that I have always been faithful to you," Santuzzo said weakly. "I beg you, Don Ciccio, help me... There must be a mistake!"

"I want to tell you a story..." said Ciccio, lighting a cigarette.

"Once upon a time, in a faraway town, there was a fisherman. Even though he wasn't rich, he lived a dignified life. One of his children, named Santuzzo, dreamed of making money, so he turned to the Corleone family…"

Ciccio began to walk around the chair as the man nervously turned his head from side to side, trying not to lose sight of him.

"He managed to be liked by this family, who put him in charge of collecting the pizzo. He would get the money, put it in a nice briefcase and give it to the cashier. The job was easy and safe. Everything went well for more than ten years…"

"It has been like that," whined Santuzzo, "and it will always be, I swear!"

A powerful slap hit him in the face, silencing him. "Never dare interrupt me, especially with lies, when I am speaking!"

The man, shaking, began uttering sentences that made no sense.

Ciccio ignored his blubbering and resumed talking: "Ten days ago, an unfortunate incident happened. His famous briefcase containing the usual five million euros in cash didn't reach the cashier, but was used instead to pay the Colombian shipment…"

Santuzzo instantly stopped mumbling.

"I wonder why our South American friends did not like the fake bills they found in the briefcase."

He brought his face closer to the man's, still tied to the chair. Ciccio could smell the fetid breath rise up to his nostrils. "Would you know anything about it?"

"N…no," stuttered the man, "nothing, I swear!"

"Niente sai—you know nothing, eh? And I bet you also know nothing of your cousin Salvatore's garage."

"My cousin?"

"Yup. And his garage, full of machinery to print fake money. Salvatore told us you often go to him."

"It is not true!" shouted Santuzzo, hysterical. "I don't know anything about it!"

"We said the same thing to the Colombians," Ciccio said, shrugging. "What do you think? Did they believe us?"

"But I..."

"Muto devi stare!" silenced Ciccio, slapping Santuzzo violently, until the restrained man spat blood. "You have no idea how much harm you have caused us because of your greed," he continued. "Two of our best men died in the shootout with the Colombians! And for what? For your fake minchia money!"

Santuzzo's face swelled, already disfigured by the beating.

"I thought you were a man, but you are a worm just like any other."

Ciccio snapped his fingers, and a large trapdoor opened in front of the prisoner's chair. Along with the unbearable stench, the grunting of dozens of pigs came from the black hole. Santuzzo wriggled desperately, trying to get up or to drop to the side.

The ropes were really tight.

"You have chosen your path," Ciccio said. "Your animal friends haven't eaten for three days. They will happily welcome you."

Three men in decorated uniforms entered the room and sat behind an imposing desk. All the military men stood up.

"The next case is about Lieutenant Ermenegildo Bertolini," one of them announced, scratching his square, white beard.

"Let the defendant rise!" ordered the second, whose head was shaved, banging his gavel on the desk.

In the front row, wearing a wide striped uniform and handcuffed, Egil obeyed. Two sinewy armed guards stood at attention next to him.

"Lieutenant Bertolini," said the last of the three men with a patch over his right eye, "you are accused of the following war crimes: abuse of power and vandalism, ill-treatment of the civilian population, and mass slaughter. What do you have to say in your defense?"

"I am innocent, Your Honor," the defendant replied, unfazed. "I have never committed the crimes I am accused of."

The shaven man continued, "You know well, Lieutenant, that we have in our possession three videos showing you committing these crimes. You have seen them also, haven't you?"

"I have, Your Honor, and I am not the person in those videos."

"Lieutenant, your position is only getting worse," the man with the white beard said. "In addition to the videos, we have testimonies of ten civilians who claim to have witnessed you committing those crimes."

"Your Honor, I have served my country with the utmost devotion and honesty," Egil retorted, resolute. "My men and my superiors know it. These false leads are part of a plot against me!"

"No one wanted to testify on your behalf, Lieutenant," sighed the other.

Egil seemed lost for a moment and then whispered: "It's impossible..."

"Lieutenant Bertolini, if today you were to plead guilty, you could get away with ten years in prison," said the shaven man. "If, however, you keep this up, you will face life in prison or worse, the death penalty."

"Think really hard about it," said the white-bearded man. "We want to help you. Plead guilty and we will be understanding. Our homeland doesn't forget its servants. You just need to admit you did wrong. Who among us has never done that?"

The entire room was holding their breath and even time seemed to stand still.

After a long pause, Egil broke the silence: "I have complete trust in the institutions—"

The man with the white beard smiled, satisfied. "You made the best choice."

"—and for this exact reason, I am sure that justice will prove my innocence!" concluded Egil, looking at the three men with defiance.

"So, you are pleading...?" stammered the shaven man, stunned.

"Innocent, Your Honor!"

A murmur made its way through the room, growing gradually in intensity.

"Silence!" shouted the third man, who wore the eye patch, banging the hammer on the desk several times.

"Having seen the evidence, heard the witnesses, and listened to the defendant's testimony, the jury will now pass its verdict."

Guilty, guilty, guilty.

"The defendant is found guilty of all charges against him. This Court sentences him to twenty-five years of strict regime prison. Court is now adjourned."

The guards urged Egil to leave the courtroom while those present showered him with whistles and heavy insults.

"I have faith in justice!" Egil shouted, shaking his head. "God knows I am innocent, and I am sure that the Court of Appeals will prove it!"

"Death! Death!" chanted those present, as Lieutenant Bertolini walked away escorted by the guards.

Sabino lifted his head from the sink and looked himself in the mirror as the water washed away the last bits of his vomit.

"What a fucking face," he thought as he looked at his reflection. "Get yourself together, S.P.! You'll make it for sure!"

The door burst open, and Gabry walked into the bathroom.

"So that's where the fuck you are! Hurry up, they're about to start!"

"I'm coming, I'm coming," replied Sabino trying to brace himself.

The place was packed. Suddenly, all the lights went out, except for those on the stage. An African American man with a shaved head made his entrance to approach the microphone. He was welcomed by a thunderous applause.

"Hello, brothers! Welcome to the Backstreet! I am Da Mastah, and you guys are awesome!"

Shouts of approval rose from the audience followed by a new roar of applause.

"Thank you! Our evening begins with a new guest, straight from Southern Italy: DJ S.P.!"

Sabino entered the stage, followed by a long clapping of hands.

"Yo, brother! Show us what you are capable of! Let's make this disco spin around!" the announcer urged him, exiting the stage as hip-hop scratches foretold the start of the performance.

Sabino felt a stab in his stomach and tried to suppress gagging. For the first time, he was all alone in front of all those people. The bass vibrations, however, dissolved all fear and he began to sing, breakdancing at the same time:

We are from Bari, oh yeah!
What do you have to say, stranger?

The audience fell silent. The spectators looked at each other, confused. Following the haunting rhythm of the base, Sabino continued:

I am coming from the best town around
the grass doesn't grow, but Baresi live there
In the whole continent we are the best
and we dance this tarantella in jest

A murmur of disapproval ran through the audience.

"What the fuck are you saying?" shouted a man.

"Go back home, terrone!" a girl insulted him at the top of her lungs.

Papers and cigarette butts were thrown on the stage, but DJ S.P. did not care:

Tòcche tòcche tòcche,
ready are the apricots
the neighbor farmer has firm ones
but I touch them not…

Sabino was showered by a bunch of garbage, amid booing and shouting. Da Mastah rushed to the stage followed by another staff member.

"Okay, okay," he announced as the music stopped abruptly. "Let's thank DJ S.P. for his exotic rap. And now, brothers, it's the fucking turn of an old acquaintance of ours: Margial M.C.!"

The audience welcomed the new singer with enthusiasm as the announcer dragged Sabino away.

When they were backstage, Da Mastah yanked Sabino hard,

slamming him to the ground. "What the fuck is wrong with you? What was that shit?"

"Your audience doesn't understand a damn thing!" Sabino replied getting up. "That is RiB, rapping in *barese*! That stuff rocks!"

"RiB? Stuff that rocks?" Da Mastah repeated, in shock. "What are you blabbering about? You are crazy, brother! You ruined my evening!"

In an instant, Sabino saw his world crashing down on him. All his beliefs, his dreams, his life…every single day spent imagining that glorious moment was turning to be a useless waste of time.

The announcer opened a back door.

"Never show your face here again! My club has a reputation to uphold!" he growled, kicking him out.

Sabino, filled with rage, clenched his knuckles, barely holding onto his temper to keep from attacking the other man.

"Get a job!" Da Mastah shouted at him. "Rap is not for you!"

With a thud, the door closed, and Sabino was left alone in the dark alley.

"Asshole!" he swore, throwing his Backstreet pass at the door. "One day I will be rich and famous, and you will beg me to give you an autograph!"

He turned around and walked down the street, leaving the club and that disappointing evening behind.

Arian, wearing a fur coat and holding a big package in her hands, rang the doorbell.

On the door, a large Christmas star lit up the entire landing. She felt a shiver ran down her spine: she hadn't been home in a very long time.

A blond woman in a blue satin robe opened the door and looked Arian up and down.

"Can I help you?" she asked coldly.

After a moment of uncertainty, Arian flashed a big smile without removing her dark glasses.

"Good evening… I am Arian, a friend of Carlo's. Is he home?"

"Hello!" the woman replied, with a friendlier tone. "I am Francesca. Please, come in. I guess you are here to discuss the solidarity dinner…"

Arian, puzzled, nodded and walked in. The furniture was different and even the way the rooms were arranged was no longer the same.

"Mom! Mom!"

As soon as she heard that little voice, Arian was hit by a hurricane of wonderful memories. A brown-haired child was walking toward her with open arms.

"Lorenzo, you rascal!" Francesca addressed the child taking him in her arms. "Tell me, what is it?"

Arian realized she was struggling to hold her tears back.

"Ma'am, are you all right?" Francesca asked her.

"Yes, thank you," she mumbled. "My apologies. I have a bad conjunctivitis, which forces me to wear sunglasses..."

"Oh, I'm sorry," replied Francesca walking the hallway to show her the way. "Carlo is in here. He is always so busy."

Arian wasn't listening to a single word; lost in her memories, she gently stroked the child's face.

"He'll turn three tomorrow," Francesca said.

"I know," replied Arian, giving the package she was holding to her. "This is a present for him!"

"Did you hear, Lorenzo? Say thank you to the lady."

The child did not stop peering at her, intrigued and at the same time intimidated by her dark glasses.

"Please, excuse us now," Francesca added. "I have meat on the stove. Come, Lorenzo, let's go! Help me cook, will you?"

As they walked away, Arian opened the door to a studio with old-fashioned furniture. Behind a desk in fine hardwood was a dark-haired man in his mid-thirties, busily typing on the keyboard of his computer.

"Please, come in," he said without looking up. "I just need two more minutes, and I'll be—"

"Carlo! It's me. I am back."

The man turned around to look at the door and saw someone he would never have thought to see again.

"Oh, my God! Is it really you?"

Arian smiled. "Yes, it is me indeed."

Carlo jumped on his feet and rushed to hug her. "My God, Marianna," he mumbled, his eyes shining. "We thought you were dead... What happened to you? Where have you been?"

"I don't feel like talking about it now. Just hug me."

"Take off your glasses," Carlo said. "I want to look you in the eyes."

Arian withdrew immediately from the hug.

"No," she replied, adamant. "I don't want you to see me. I am hideous."

"What are you saying?" he replied, confused. "And this scary ring? You never had it before. Where did you get it?"

Carlo tried to remove her silver ring with the eye carved within a triangle. He did not succeed.

"Let's just say that it is a part of me now," Arian trying to brush his concerns aside. "I never take it off."

Carlo paled and stepped back toward the desk. With a swift movement, he detached the symbol of the Church Dei Invicti Operae from the wall: the Latin cross within the Star of David.

"What's the matter with you?" Arian asked him, shocked.

"You are not Marianna!" the man shouted, frantically dialing a phone number as he pointed the object at her. "You are a damned Luciferal in the body of my ex-wife."

"It is me! Can't you see it? Stop!"

"Police? Come, quick! There is a Luciferal in my home looking like my ex-wife!"

"No!" cried Arian, desperate.

Carlo looked at her with disdain, piercing her with his eyes, as if they were an icy blade. "Soon the Chrismatics will be here. It is the end for you. Go away! Leave!"

With a sob, Arian ran away, without turning around to see Francesca and Lorenzo, who were looking at her in disbelief. She ran as fast as she could, pursued by the sound of sirens. She ran through streets and squares, no rest, no destination. Finally exhausted, she fell to her knees on a field, in the darkness of the night. She struggled to take off her silver ring, and when she couldn't, she screamed in frustration.

She was sobbing now that everything she had fought for had been taken from her. She took one of her guns out and brought it slowly to her temple.

"No more fighting, no more suffering, no more sacrifices, no more…"

She pulled the trigger. Peace, finally.

XXII

Taro and Egil jolted awake as the sound of a gunshot echoed in the distance. Both were lying on the ground.

"What the fuck?" cursed Taro, getting up.

"Everything okay?" Egil asked, also getting on his feet.

"Meh. So so…"

Taro looked around: they were in the center of a big, square-shaped stone room. On the wall facing them, an imposing metal door gleamed in the flickering light of two torches.

"Where are we?" he asked, confused. "The last thing I remember is that fucking goat plunging us underground…"

Focusing, Taro tried to put into focus vague memories of a missed audience and a failed concert. His memories, though, dissolved like dreams at dawn.

"Hey, over there!"

Taro looked where his friend was pointing. On the wall to the right of the door, there was a golden statue, depicting a tall and massive man lighting a cigarette. Two big golden pigs by his legs completed the statue.

"Uagliò!" Taro said with a low whistle. "It looks exactly like Ciccio!"

"Yes, it looks a lot like him," Egil observed, kneeling to get a better look at the motionless figure. "What does it say down here?"

On the pedestal, the word CARITAS was engraved in large letters.

The boy shook his head. "Caritas? Never heard of it! Anyway, it looks like the work of a really fine artist!"

"Oh my God!" said Egil, widening his eyes.

In front of the opposite wall, there was another golden statue: a woman with long braids, kneeling and holding a gun to her temple.

"But… Don't tell me that…"

Taro ran toward the sculpture. The braided hair completely covered the woman's face, making her unrecognizable.

"It looks just like Arian," pondered Egil, joining him. "But the pose… No, it can't be her."

On the pedestal of this statue, engraved in big letters, was the word, SPES.

Taro pointed at the statue's finger depicting a ring with an eye within a triangle. "And this then? The statue is really her, there is no doubt! I don't like any of this one bit… Where are the real Ciccio and Arian?"

"After John saved us," Egil replied, "we walked into the castle, but I don't remember much more. It is as if I had strange dreams, and then voilà, I was here. That's all!"

Taro looked at the walls around them. "We are inside the castle for sure. Maybe Ciccio and Arian are around here, somewhere…" He grinned at Egil. "I hope our statues are here, too! I really want to see what I look like."

As Taro spoke, Egil walked to the metal door. It looked like it was the only way out. There were no windows, no clues indicating passageways of any kind.

"Are you ready, Taro?" his friend asked him. Taro gave a short nod.

As soon as Egil touched the knob, the door swung open, letting a blinding light flood the stone room. Taro and Egil, dazed and with half-closed eyes, heard a roar of applause.

"Here they are, fellow viewers!" announced a voice on the microphone. "They are finally here!"

Gradually, Taro got used to the strong light and looked around. They were at the top of a white staircase around which dozens and dozens of people were gathered. As two energetic men closed the red satin doors behind them, a pair of skimpily dressed valets took them under their arms, winking.

"Come on down, boys!" The voice belonged to a man wearing a blue jacket full of rhinestones. "The jury is almost done voting. I remind those who are watching us from home to call the number below. Press 'One' for Sabino Pignataro or 'Two' for Ermenegildo Bertolini!"

Prompted by the handsome valets, Taro began to walk down the stairs, utterly shocked by the entire situation. Egil, also confused, did the same. The crowd clapped and yelled their names. Some even tried desperately to touch them.

"Uagliò, this is so cool!" said Taro, posing like a star. "Yo, amicos! You are awesome! You are wonderful! An autograph? Why not two?"

Egil looked around suspiciously. "This is impossible… This can't be possible…"

The man with the blue jacket joined them, standing between the two Martyrs.

"This is the most important moment of the show," he announced with emphasis, as the lights were turned off. "The jury is ready to officially announce the winner of the first season of this wonderful program that has kept young and old alike glued to the screen for months: *Sancta Sanctorum*!"

A new wave of applause followed the man's words, and the host bestowed the crowd with a beaming smile.

"Wait!" Egil's peremptory tone caused silence to fall among the crowd. "Can someone explain to me what is happening?"

"That's it, fellow viewers!" the announcer exclaimed. "As you can see, it's all true! Up until now, none of them knew they were contestants."

"Meaning?"

"It is simple. When you passed the auditions to participate in *Sancta Sanctorum: The Quest for the Holy Grail*, you signed a release, and then you underwent a special hypnosis session."

"Hypnosis?" Taro repeated. "Why?"

"Our expert of the subconscious will be happy to answer your question: Dr. Nuzzi! Let's give him a round of applause!"

From the first row of chairs, a bald man in his sixties found himself in the spotlight of a bull's-eye. He stood and waved at the crowd.

"Good evening, everyone!" he began. "So, why a hypnosis session? The participants go through seemingly risky competitions, meant to bring the best out of them. In order not to distort their behaviors or reactions, it is necessary for the contestant to believe that they are truly experiencing each dangerous situation. Only this way are we certain that they are not faking their kindness or purity in order to win the final prize."

"So, everything we experienced so far was fake?" asked Taro doubtfully.

"More or less," replied the presenter. "The difficulties were real, but you never risked getting seriously hurt or dying. *Sancta Sanctorum*'s trials are hard, but our group of experts in special effects, together with the Union of Volunteer Rescuers, made sure that nothing ever happened to you. Right?"

Taro nodded. He had to acknowledge that he was, indeed, feeling great.

"Good. So, the jury has made its decision. Now we will know the official results."

The solemn tone of the man with the blue jacket had completely captured the audience's attention. The room turned silent. Taro instinctively crossed his fingers.

One of the assistants handed a sealed envelope to the host. He opened it with studied slowness to increase the effect of suspense.

"The winner of the first season of *Sancta Sanctorum*..."

Taro closed his eyes as his heart raced with excitement.

"...Sabino Pignataro!"

The orchestra played a triumphant march as colorful confetti rained down profusely amid the applause.

"Yay!"

Sabino jumped up and down with joy while Egil stood motionless, his eyes staring into the void.

The host congratulated Sabino, shaking his hand: "Here is your prize: the Holy Grail!"

Swaying her hips sensuously, the valet arrived on the stage, pushing a crystal cart on which towered a solid gold cup, artfully engraved and historiated, like art on the pages of a medieval manuscript.

"Listen to me," said Egil, putting a hand on Sabino's shoulder. "This is not the Holy Grail we are looking for. Please, let's get out of here."

"Get over it, bro!" replied Sabino triumphant. "Didn't you get it yet? This is the truth. All the other things we believed in are all bullshit! We've been hypnotized!"

The assistants took Egil under their arms, inviting him to leave Sabino alone on the stage.

"Come on!" Egil pleaded.

"You come on! Relax!" replied Sabino, stroking the golden cup. "This is the Holy Grail! Look at it: it is here, finally!"

Suddenly, six energetic men grabbed Egil and dragged him away.

"Let me go!" he shouted as he disappeared backstage. "Taro! Don't stay here!"

"Is there any way to bring him to his senses?" asked Sabino to the presenter.

"Dr. Nuzzi will take care of him immediately," the smiling man assured him. "Don't worry."

Sabino lifted the Holy Grail up high, under the photographers' flashes, kissed by the two sexy valets. What more could he ask for of his life?

XXIII

Castel del Monte (Andria)

"Taro, let's leave!"

Egil jolted awake. The bitter cold penetrated his bones.

"Welcome," greeted a voice. "It's an honor for me to meet you, George."

Egil pulled himself up. He was in a large octagonal courtyard covered in snow. As the snowflakes fell, a hooded figure in a red cloak walked toward him, leaning against his curved crosier.

"My name is Egil. And you? Who are you?"

"You say your name is Egil, but I sense in you the Spirit of Saint George. I can clearly hear the roar of the dragon shaking the foundation of this castle…"

"Saint George is always with me: he guides and protects me," said Egil brushing his dragon-shaped pendant. "But tell me your name. I feel I know you."

When he was just a few steps away from him, the mysterious man threw back his hood. A flowing beard and long white hair framed a face with a dark complexion, marked by years.

"Yes, I know you! You are… Saint Nicholas!"

"I must compliment you, because your soul is pure," the Saint said, smiling benevolently. "God's grace lives in you, and you have proved yourself worthy to host the saint who protects you, unlike your companions."

"What do you mean?" Egil asked, his voice dry with worry. "Where are my friends?"

"See for yourself," replied Nicholas, pointing to a spot behind him.

Egil turned around, and in the center of a big opening leading to the castle, he saw a golden statue. It depicted Taro, who was lifting a trophy to the sky while two beautiful girls kissed him on each cheek. On the pedestal was engraved in big letters the word FIDES. The statues of Ciccio and Arian sparkled on the way inside the castle.

"Rejoice! You are the only one who managed to cross the three barriers I erected to protect the castle."

"So, the statues… Is it really them?"

"More precisely, each statue is what is left of their body," Nicholas answered. "When a spirit isn't pure enough to pass the test of Virtue, its body gets transformed into a statue that will stay here forever."

Nicholas tapped his knuckles on Taro's silhouette and continued, "Do you hear? Outside, the statue is beautiful, but inside it is empty. So were they: outwardly pure and incorruptible, but, without the grace of God, empty inside."

Egil looked him straight in the eyes. "I feel it is a bit too hasty and definitive a judgment. After all, we are human beings…"

"Do you mean to say that Ciccio was an example of mercy and love for others? Or worse, Sabino? Do you think he had an unshakable faith?" Nicholas scoffed. "Forget them. Your spirit is that of a saint. You are now above human imperfections."

"Forget my friends?" Egil demanded, surrounded by a crimson aura. "Never! I won't go anywhere without them!"

The aura vanished. The knight wore his armor and held his spear.

"The dragon's blood is boiling in your veins," Nicholas observed, "but unfortunately your anger won't change things."

Spreading his arms wide, the Saint was enveloped by a golden light, which took on a triangular shape. At each vertex of the triangle shone a glowing sphere.

"Each of them chose their own destiny. You must come to terms with it."

Egil tightened his grip on his weapon. He thought of each statue, and that increased his sadness and anger. He stretched out his left arm and withdrew his right one, holding the spear, ready to hurl it at the enemy. Thoughts of the sculptures of his friends overlapped with the memories of the massacre of his soldiers. He had been unable to protect them then. This time he would not allow the same fate to befall them.

"Calm down!" ordered Nicholas, walking with open arms under the falling snow. "Don't let anger blind your faith. I won't fight a spirit as pure as yours. It would not be fair. Think about this: our fight would benefit only the Luciferals."

Hearing those words, Egil hesitated, even though in his heart the roar of the dragon, eager to fight, was vibrating. Just then, a strong earth tremor shook the entire castle, as deep as its own foundations, and a crevasse opened in the courtyard.

The two lost their balance, as a huge black beast with three canine heads and white eyes jumped out from the huge hole. Its long spiky tail lashed the air menacingly.

One glace was enough for them to understand each other: that conversation could wait.

Egil leapt to his feet and sprinted toward the creature. With skilled lunges, he was able to hold off the heads, which emitted terrible howls and tried to bite him. Suddenly, however, a pair of jaws clamped down on the spear, tossing it away. Disarmed, Egil had to roll on the ground several times to avoid being crushed under the monster's paws.

The three heads, relentless, stretched one more time toward him. Just when it was about to strike, the creature was blocked by a huge crosier. Screaming in pain, it opened its jaws to let the weapon drop. Nicholas's crosier returned to its normal size.

"Quick, pick up your spear!" shouted Nicholas, retrieving his own weapon.

Egil nodded and ran breathlessly under the falling snowflakes. He could feel the beast growling just behind him. Once he found his spear, he turned around to look at the fight: the beast was pawing the Saint.

"In nominee Patris…"

Immediately, the creature's entire paw turned into gold, making the demon lose its balance. It fell on its side. But the three-headed beast did not give up and tried an even stronger blow with its other extremity.

"Et Filii…" continued Nicholas, transforming the other paw. He immediately moved to the right side of the beast, followed by two of its three heads, jaws wide open.

"...Et Spiritus Sancti!"

With his crosier, the man touched both heads, instantly turning them to gold.

The monster vibrated a powerful thump of its tail creating a vigorous displacement of air.

"... Amen!" he concluded, pressing the crosier on the spiky tail.

Egil ran back to him. The monstrous dog could no longer move. The only head still alive was barking furiously, trying in vain to bite them.

"I am the defender of this castle," Nicholas declared as the golden light surrounding him became stronger. "Dark creature, I repel you in the name of God, his son Jesus, and the Holy Spirit. Go back to your abyss!"

The creature began to convulse as black smoke poured out of its eyes. Suddenly, from its open jaws came a wave of light blue energy that struck the Saint full force. When it ceased, there remained only a white statue of Nicholas, surrounded by three golden spheres.

The smoke evaporated and the last head revived immediately. Egil did not give up. He moved past the sculpture and jumped, clutching his spear in his hands. With a terrible cry, he plunged it into the monster's forehead with as much force as he could—but he felt his blood freeze in his veins when he realized the creature's hide was impenetrable.

The beast flailed and threw him off. As soon as Egil touched the ground, a fine gold dust began to fall from the animal's body. Its tail resumed wagging, and its paws regained their vigor, recovering their original color.

Staring at the monster and clutching his spear, Egil decided to try everything. For his slaughtered soldiers... In memory of his friends... For Nicholas's courage... Egil's faith would triumph!

He ran toward the demon as his blood pounded his temples. He dodged the sharp claws with a jump and lunged himself toward the belly of the monster. And then, without even a second's delay, he thrust his spear into its chest. The creature, though, did not budge; howling purposefully, the beast collapsed to the ground, crushing Egil beneath it.

It was then that three gunshots were heard. In need of air, Egil felt an intense heat on his skin. The dog was burning at the same speed fire burns paper. In a flash, it became a pool of dark, foul-smelling slime.

"Egil!" shouted three voices in unison.

He tried to get up, but excruciating pain told him he no longer had a single healthy bone. He wasn't even able to turn his head; he could only stare at the snow falling down until three familiar faces appeared in front of his eyes.

"Oh, my God!" said Arian, slowly taking his helmet off.

"Minchia, picciò!" Ciccio said. "You don't look so good."

"Hang in there!" added Taro, taking out of his pocket a vial full of manna. "Here, drink this. You can do it! Don't give up!"

The dense liquid oozed from the vial and into Egil's slightly parted lips. He immediately regained color.

"Guys!" he coughed. "It is so wonderful to see you again!"

"How are you feeling?" asked Arian.

"I feel great," he replied, getting up as a crimson light enveloped him entirely.

"Sticazzi!" cursed Taro, observing in awe first his friend, and then the empty vial of manna. "This thing is really cool!"

"How the hell did you defeat the Luciferal?" Egil asked them. "My spear only tickled it!"

"Check for yourself," replied Arian, pointing to the monster's remains.

Egil turned around. Where there had been a pool of dark ooze before, there were now three small objects glowing between the flames.

"It's Aurum," the woman explained, satisfied.

"Where did you find it?"

"It was my humble idea!" said Taro, proudly. "We found ourselves here in this square, under the snow, in front of the white statue of Saint Nicholas."

"You must have been released from your statues when the Luciferal disabled Nicholas," Egil mused.

Taro just shrugged. "Anyway, his statue had three beautiful golden orbs around it! I remembered the conversations on alchemy, and I thought: 'Now I'll show that Luciferal!' So, while the others did not know what to do, I soaked the orbs with holy water and then..."

"Slow down, picciò! I was the one who turned the three orbs into bullets. Otherwise, now, you would be juggling in front of the monster's heads, lo capisti?"

"If I were you, I would thank the aim of a certain person who scored three centers out of three," Arian added.

Egil laughed. "You acted like a team of close-knit professionals. Congratulations to you all. Bishop Grassano would be proud of you."

"Yeah," teased Ciccio, "next time I see him, I will make sure to let him know how it went today and finally he'll understand that we work better without you!"

"Well, now let's finish playing," Egil said, brushing himself off. "Let's find the Holy Grail and get out of here!"

XXIV

Castel del Monte (Andria)

White snowflakes fell silently from the sky.

"Hey, guys!" exclaimed Taro, pointing to a specific spot. "Look there!"

The bullets made of Aurum had turned again into three bright golden orbs and were rolling in single file toward the statue of Saint Nicholas. Once they reached their destination, two stopped at the sides of the pedestal while the third moved up, in the center. They formed a sort of triangle.

"Maybe it's a sign," said Ciccio. "Maybe Nicholas is trying to tell us that the Holy Grail is there, under him."

Egil shook his head.

Arian suggested having a look. "And let's get the orbs back. They'll surely come in handy," she added, pushing an unruly red wisp of hair from her face.

Ciccio bent down to grab one of the mysterious objects, but soon found that it didn't budge. While Arian and Egil tried to help him, Taro made his way to the edge of the hole from which the three-headed monster had emerged. For some absurd reason, he felt drawn to the crevasse. He carefully leaned over and waited for his eyes to adjust to the darkness. Many feet below, there lay a cross and an altar.

"Guys! I think I found a clue!"

Arian joined him, and immediately the boy showed her the inside of the hole. "Don't they look like the remains of a church to you?"

"It could very well be the Church of Santa Maria del Monte!"

Suddenly, the snowfall stopped. From above, a powerful wind blew over the courtyard, sweeping everything away. The violent gusts made Arian lose her balance, sending her tumbling over the edge.

"Arian!"

Taro grabbed her hand. Lying on the loose snow, he dug his feet into the ground until he felt some friction. He would not be able to lift her up by himself, but he would hold on until Egil and Ciccio arrived to help.

"Servants of the Anti-Christ, your time has come!" thundered a familiar voice.

"What's happening?" asked Arian, concerned, her feet dangling in the air.

Taro turned around and saw that, amid the snow vortex, stood the proud figure of Augustine, riding his winged bull. "This time you will not escape the wrath of the Almighty!" the Saint added smugly.

His steed immediately folded its white wings and, as if by magic, the fury of the wind stopped. The Saint dismounted and noticed the statue of the castle guardian.

"You damned heretics!" he shouted filled with rage. "You dared lift your bloody fist even against Nicholas!"

"Wait," protested Egil. "This isn't our fault! It was a Luciferal."

"Shut up, you despicable being!" Augustine admonished him. "I hope the Almighty will have mercy on you, because I will have none!"

The winged bull began to swipe its right foot on the ground, pointing its horns toward the two Martyrs. Taro's hands were sweaty. He did not know how much longer he would be able to hold Arian. He prayed for his friends to get rid of the enemy as quickly as possible.

"Go!" Augustine shouted.

The animal launched itself headlong at Egil and Ciccio as the earth shook under its weight.

Egil rolled to the side, surrounded by crimson light. A moment later, he rose to his feet, wrapped in his gleaming armor. Ciccio turned into a lion with a thick mane and dodged the attack. When the bull turned around to face him, he indulged in a powerful roar. The two beasts began to circle around, exchanging defiant looks.

The Saint approached the knight. "Now you will suffer the torments you deserve for your wicked acts!" he announced, disarming the Martyr with the lower part of the crosier. With the curved end, however, he grabbed Egil's neck.

Egil fell to his knees in the snow. He tried to free himself from the relentless grip of the staff, but the crosier, like a snake, tightened more and more around his throat.

"Are you in pain, you damned heretic? And this is just the beginning! Now you will suffer the torments of the divine scourge!"

Augustine raised his right hand to the sky, and as he closed his fingers, a large, spiked whip appeared in his fist. He struck a powerful lash against the Martyr. The whip cut through Egil's armor as if it were butter. The cord struck him several times, causing him to spit blood.

Egil never lowered his head. "You can scourge my body all you want, but you will never be able to put out the fire of myfaith!"

At that moment, the body of the big, winged bull plummeted down beside them. Red dyed the snow around its head. The lion, wounded in one paw, came to meet them. It had managed to rip open the back of the bull's head with its fangs.

"It can't be…" muttered the Saint, dumbfounded.

Taro looked at Arian again, hopeful. "Hang in there, Arian. Help is almost here!"

His arms were sore, and his feet kept on slipping. But soon his friends would arrive to help him. He had faith.

Arian shook her head. She could feel his weariness. "Let me go and run to help them. I'll be fine," she said turning to look at the remains of the church below.

"No way!" retorted Taro, tightening his grip.

"Damn them!" shouted Augustine from across the courtyard.

Taro looked in the direction of the enemy and saw the bull take his last breath, lying in the Saint's arms. Egil, crawling through the snow, had managed to retrieve his own spear. The lion was next to him, proud and wounded.

"In the name of God, I condemn you to eternal suffering!"

Two bright golden globes appeared on Augustine's palms, which turned into flaming hearts. The two Martyrs collapsed to the ground. Ciccio roared, writhing in the snow, while the knight slumped down with his eyes wide open.

"Amen!" concluded the man, closing his hands into fists.

Distraught, Taro did not even have time to notice that he had slipped over the edge.

At the bottom of the crevasse, the wind lashed Arian's face. She was lying on the bare stone. The entire right side of her body ached. Beside her, Taro was opening his eyes after the fall. A huge underground cavern opened around them, barely illuminated by the dim light filtering through the crevasse.

"Are you all right?" Arian asked, stroking the boy's head. Taro blushed.

Silence.

"Can you hear me?" she insisted, lightly slapping his face.

"Yes... I'm fine!" replied Taro, sitting up. He looked upward, facing the opening above his head. Not a sound, not a snowflake came down from up there.

As always, Arian knew his thoughts. "There is no way to go back up. We must continue the search for the Holy Grail ourselves. That's the best way to help them."

"But..."

"Look! There are torches there!"

The woman pulled out a lighter from her pocket, and soon the cave was lit by three small flames. A few wooden benches were rotting on the floor, and ancient, sacred furniture decorated a dusty altar, where there was a painting depicting the Virgin Mary. Embedded in the rock floor was a wooden Latin cross, six feet long, untouched by the wear and tear of time.

"And that writing? What does it mean?" asked Taro massaging his head.

Arian noticed that next to the cross there was an epigraph engraved on a marble slab.

"It is Greek," she explained to him, kneeling down to read. "It says something like this: 'He who with a sincere heart yearns for communion will set out on the road traveled by the Savior. Following his shining example, he will become one with the Blood of Christ.'"

"This again?"

"It looks like it…"

"What else does it say?"

"Just a sec Taro. There are still two lines left…"

"Okay, okay, take your time."

Out of the corner of her eye, Arian noticed that Taro was looking at the sky again. He was worried for Egil and Ciccio. She, too, felt the anguish tighten her stomach. But the Holy Grail was too close to forget their mission now. Suddenly, Taro's face turned into pure terror.

"Watch out!"

He pushed Arian onto her painful right side, away from the cross. Moments later, a man in armor descended from above and pierced Taro's chest with a spear. The boy slumped on the ground, motionless, as a trickle of blood ran from his mouth. Arian, distraught, pointed her guns to the attacker, ready to shoot.

"Don't do it!"

She gasped, hearing that unexpected voice. In front of her flickered the image of a woman holding a palm branch: it was Lucy.

"Listen to me! It is better not to attack this man now," said the Saint with motherly warmth, vanishing at once in a flash of light.

The attacker was tall and wore the typical outfit of ancient Roman legionaries: segmented armor, red cloak, tunic, sandals, and a cingulum where a saddleback, a sword, and a dagger hung. He had black eyes and salt and pepper hair, just like his beard.

"Who are you, wretched one?" Arian demanded.

"My name is Longinus," he explained, walking toward her. "I am the protector of the Holy Blood on behalf of his Most Excellent Holiness."

"Stop! I have you at gunpoint."

"You poor deluded soul!" Longinus chuckled. "Look, this is what happens to those who try to thwart the justice of the Almighty."

The legionnaire pulled something out of his saddlebag and threw it to the ground: it was a severed head.

Arian shuddered, recognizing it. "John!"

With a surprising sprint, Longinus drew his dagger and lunged at her, following the blow with an upward slice of his sword. Arian danced swiftly between the blades, avoiding both blows. Survival instincts asserted themselves, and a shot went off from one of the guns, directed at the legionnaire's left knee.

"Aaah!"

It was Taro's voice. Incredulous, Arian turned around to see with horror that Taro's left knee was bleeding, but that their enemy's remained untouched.

"As you see, evil always turns in on itself," Longinus said.

The bandana around Taro's wrist glowed. Abruptly, he sat up and his hands grabbed the spear piercing his chest. He closed his eyes, inhaling deeply. "With one swift movement he will remove it," thought Arian hopeful.

Taro opened his eyes wide. A trickle of blood gushed from his mouth. He had drawn out the spear only a few inches.

"I am sorry, Anti-Christ," Longinus commented, "not even your exceptional power can do anything against the Spear of Destiny! Its tip binds itself firmly with the soul of the enemy and inflicts whatever damage is done to me."

Arian winced. She understood then Lucy's words: to strike Longinus would mean to injure Taro.

Augustine's fingers curled, his power penetrating the two Martyr's flaming hearts, piercing them with his nails.

Suddenly, the lion lying in the snow turned into a huge leech, a creature without a real heart.

"It is not possible!" the Saint said, as the two organs pulverized under his eyes.

A golden orb appeared in the palm of his left hand, but this time it did not turn into a burning heart. With a flick the leech sprang forward and pounced on his chest. Without his lifeblood, Augustine began to shrivel as the beast grew bigger and bigger.

His voice came out faintly from his wracked lips. "Damn you…"

He collapsed to the ground, shriveled like a mummy. The creature broke away slithering toward Egil, who remained unconscious. Once the leech reached his side, it turned into Ciccio, who tried to hoist Egil up onto his shoulder.

"Minchia, you are heavy!" he huffed. "Amunìnne, picciò, wake up! We need to look for Arian and Taro! Wake up!"

Ciccio slapped him on the cheeks, but seeing that the technique wasn't working, he was overtaken by a horrific doubt and put two fingers on Egil's neck, just below the jawline.

No heart beating. Without hesitation, Ciccio brought his ear close to his friend's mouth. No breathing, either.

Longinus launched himself again at Arian, who gracefully avoided each blow.

"My compliments, faithless bitch," he said, sheathing his sword and dagger. "I can see you are skillful, just like any other devil-worshipping heathen."

"You are wrong," she replied. "We just want to save humankind from Armageddon. The Devil is also an enemy of ours! Fighting us means favoring the Luciferals!"

"Shut up!" Longinus growled back. "Your lies offend the sacredness of this place."

With a quick movement, he took some objects from his saddlebag and threw them in the air.

"Crucifige!" he cried, making the sign of the cross.

Before she could defend herself from the attack, she was nailed to the cave's wall by four thunderbolts. She screamed until her throat scraped raw. Her wrists and ankles had been pierced.

"You fucking bastard!" shouted Taro, trying again to pull out the Spear of Destiny.

He threw up blood again.

"No!" Arian warned him, trying to free herself. "Don't, or you will die!"

"Arian…" Taro whispered, with tears in his eyes. He glowed of the whitest of light. "I don't want to see you die… And there is only one way to save you…"

"No! Don't do it! I beg you!"

Taro tightened his grip around the spear. A cascade of blood accompanied the spike's exit from his chest. He fell backward on the wooden cross embedded on the floor.

The other Martyr, desperate, lowered her head to avoid the sight. A grin of sadistic satisfaction appeared on Longinus's face.

"This is the fate awaiting those who turn their backs on the Light."

Arian kept her head down, her breath pitched as though she were holding back tears.

"You must look!"

Longinus grabbed her by her braids, yanking her head backward.

Then abruptly he took off her sunglasses.

What he saw shocked him so much that he began to shake. He cried in terror, and his face morphed into pain. And then a heavy unnatural silence fell. In place of Longinus was now a black marble statue, depicting him in the act of covering his eyes with his hands.

The four nails fell to the ground, freeing Arian. She picked up her sunglasses and put them on again. She walked slowly to Taro. He was lying in a lake of blood, arms outstretched over the large cross. He had the serene expression of a sleeping child.

"Why did you do that? Why?" the woman said sobbing.

When she said those words, the bandana began to glow. Independently, it untied itself from Taro's wrist and grew until it became a white sheet that wrapped itself gently around the lifeless body of its Martyr.

The walls of the cave and of the castle began to glow. Soon, the whole valley lit brightly. At the top of the hill shone a sort of octagonal sun.

The light vanished, taking with it the castle. Slowly the snow stopped, and the horizon became pink.

XXV

Castel del Monte (Andria)

Egil opened his eyes and realized that Ciccio's lips were on his. He pushed him away immediately, coughing.

"Praise the heavens!" said Ciccio, drenched in sweat. "You are alive!"

"More or less," Egil replied noticing he was not only without his armor, but also shirtless. "I feel bruised all over my chest…"

"Minchia, it's been ages since the last time I did CPR. I guess I overdid it."

"But where are we? Weren't we at the castle?"

"Until a few minutes ago we were, yes," Ciccio agreed. "But while I was reviving you, all the walls lit up, and I had to close my eyes because it was too bright. When I opened them again, the castle was gone."

Egil could not believe such an incredible disappearance. There was no trace left of the castle. Surprised, he noticed Nicholas's statue behind him. That immediately spurred traumatic memories.

"Shit!" he cursed, bringing his hand to his chest. "Augustine… What happened to him?"

"Don't worry, picciò." Ciccio pointed to a shrunken mummy. "He can no longer bother us. But tell me, can you get up?"

Egil sat up. "Where are Arian and Taro?"

"I don't know," Ciccio replied, exhaling the smoke from his cigarette, his eyes lost on the horizon. "As soon as you can manage, we will go look for them."

Egil strained his ear. In the distance a woman's wails could be heard. "Listen! Can you hear that?"

Ciccio stood in silence, smoke curling up from his cigarette.

"Pay attention," Egil insisted, slowly rising to his feet. He walked toward the other side of the hill, followed by Ciccio. After a few steps, he saw Arian, kneeling in front of a black marble statue. She was crying.

As soon as they were next to her, their friend stood and threw herself into the knight's arms, sobbing.

"Guys…it is so nice to see you again!"

"Minchia!" said Ciccio. He was looking at a large wooden cross. Right in its center, a golden object sparkled under the first dawn.

"But this is…" Egil muttered. His words died out. It was an octagonal cup, like its supporting foot. Its exterior was studded with precious stones, and inside it was enameled dark red.

Arian finished the sentence for him: "The Holy Grail… It looks like the castle!"

“Perfeita intuition,” said a solemn voice.

The three turned around and saw Saint Anthony walking toward them, with the blond child in his arms.

“Hi Everyone! La voz de Deus urged me to come here to quell the bellicose spirits. But I am too late, I am afraid…”

Egil interrupted him to ask Arian where the fourth member of their group was.

Crushed by the weight of the sentence she was about to say, Arian lowered her head.

“Taro…is dead.”

“What?” said Egil and Ciccio at the same time.

Arian told them what had happened, looking at the black marble statue. “He sacrificed himself for me. He decided to die to allow me to defeat Longinus. It is all my fault. I should have protected him!”

Egil held her close, stroking her hair. Thinking that the boy was no longer with them made his eyes moisten. Ciccio took out a pair of dark glasses from the breast pocket of his suit and put them on. Without saying a word, he sat down, placed the Holy Grail on the cross, where it had been before, and lit another cigarette.

The blond child whispered something into Anthony’s ear.

“Rejoice, people!” the Saint exclaimed.

Everyone turned around toward him, surprised.

“Our jovem has performed a noble heroic deed. Even if you can’t see him, he is here now, close to us.”

"Cut it out, Don Anthony," huffed Ciccio, annoyed. "I can't stand this kind of preaching."

"He will always be next to you," Anthony continued, "and he will protect you, in communion with the Holy Grail, amèm and amen!"

Those words left the three Martyrs astonished. They stared at the golden Grail.

"'He who seeks communion with the Holy Grail shall follow the path trodden by Christ…'" whispered Arian, remembering the words of Joseph of Arimathea.

"Minchia, I understand!" said Ciccio, clapping a hand on his forehead. "Taro chose to sacrifice himself, just like Christ did centuries ago."

Smiling, the child Anthony held clapped his hands.

"You are right," Arian reflected. "It was Taro's noble deed that made the miracle happen. Right before my eyes, the Holy Grail, hidden for centuries under the appearances of a castle, came in communion with him and returned to its original form! I should have realized this earlier."

"Làgrimas often prevent faith from illuminating the visão," commented the Saint. Arian's hand rose to cover her face, taking his words of wisdom literally.

Egil picked up the Grail and looked inside. He was amazed to see an image of Taro with his thumb raised.

"Adeus, my heroic friends," Anthony took his leave. "La voz de Deus is calling me elsewhere. Please, guard the Holy Grail wisely for the good of all humanidade."

The three Martyrs watched the friar's silhouette walk away until he disappeared in the forest around the hill.

"Okay, guys," Egil said. "It hasn't been easy, but from now on things will get even more difficult. Our mission goes on!"

"Don't worry, picciò!" Ciccio said. "Minchia, when the going gets tough, let the tough get going! Am I right, Arian?"

"Absolutely!" replied the woman with a smile. "We are going to be great!"

The Holy Grail sparkled in the sunlight and brightened the faces of the three Martyrs, united and more determined than ever.

No matter what they had to sacrifice, they would save the world.

ABOUT THE AUTHORS

Gilbert Gallo

Like any self-respecting superhero, Gilbert Gallo, a writer, game designer, and videogames writer, has a dual identity, too. During the day, thanks to his healing superpowers, he restores smiles to those who have lost them. At night, he creates fantastic universes in which incredible characters live amazing adventures. He has dedicated himself for several years to writing manuals, settings, and adventures for roleplaying games. Now he works for different Italian and foreign publishers as a freelance, both in the field of roleplaying and board games. He has written more than fifty manuals in different languages. He has also frequently been invited to American conventions as the Italian Role Playing Game ambassador, including to the 2018 GenghisCon41 in Denver (Colorado), the 2019 GenghisCon42, and the 2020 Savage Cruise in the Caribbean Sea.

In the field of short stories and novels, he has published The Legend of Heracles vol I- Escape to Delphi and The Legend of Heracles vol II- The Kingdom of the Sphinx for Delos Digital; and contributed a story to the Land of the Anunnaki anthology for Italian Sword and Sorcery. He also writes stories for video games / mobile apps, such as Heracles, Birth of a Hero for Infinity Mundi and Pirates of Donkey Island for Choice of Games's Hosted Games.

Giulia De Gasperi

Giulia De Gasperi is a freelance editor and literary translator. Born in Italy, she has lived in Canada, Scotland, and the USA. She now splits her time between North Carolina and Ireland. Giulia loves to read, and collects picture books.